Inked Memories

PG Forte

Copyright © 2014 PG Forte

Chapultepec Press
ISBN: 978-1-880370-23-0

Praise for Inked Memories:

When PG Forte asked me to read and review her little novella called Inked Memories. I was excited. I love tattoos and artists. What I didn't expect was the emotional rollercoaster I was agreeing to... Even if you're not a fan of tattoo stories, read this. The message encased in the novella is so much more than simply getting a tattoo. It's about accepting life's surprises and learning to move on.

Turn the Page Book Reviews

I've said it before, but it bears repeating- P.G. Forte is one of those authors that everybody should know about. I've yet to read anything by her that I haven't loved and, in the case of Inked Memories, that's really saying something. Why? Because I don't usually read or enjoy novellas. There is just not enough time in the book to get to know and care about the characters or their relationships. That was not the case with this book. I loved Sophie and Declan. Their story, especially Sophie's, was really believable.

Tara Clegg

This is not my first encounter with PG Forte but it is the first time I cried while reading a story. This story was not just about two people rekindling a romance; it's about overcoming losing a part of you... Reading the previous stories in the Anthology I was expecting a hot and steamy read but I was happily surprised to have my heart squeezed in the middle of this Antho. Thank you PG.

Charity Costa, Literal Addiction

Dedication

For Dawn

Acknowledgements

The author would like to thank Kim Brooks for finding the problem with the opening; Kelly Jamieson and Erin Nicholas for providing encouragement, emotional support, camaraderie, and wine at the best writers' retreat ever; Kinsey W. Holly for making sure the New Orleans details were correct; and Dillon Forte for ensuring that the tattoo details were accurate. Any mistakes made on either of those counts, are solely the fault of the author. Finally special thanks to my wonderful editor, Devin Govaere.

Chapter One

*"If the last few years had taught Sophie anything,
it was that life was uncertain and one should always eat dessert
first."*

Early December…

The café's owner must have seen her coming. Rousseau
had Sophie's usual order — iced coffee and a chocolate
caramel roll — all ready and waiting when she walked
through the door of Café Bwe. She smiled her thanks then
quickly took her food back outside to her usual table on the
banquette. She never ate inside if she could help it. That man
was simply too gorgeous for anyone's peace of mind —
whether they were male or female. If she sat inside, she'd
only end up drooling over him. Once again she found
herself wondering how much truth there was to the rumors
about him.

She'd heard it said his touch was magic, that his sexual
healing could cure whatever ailed you, whether physical or
emotional or anything in between. It had been awhile,
however, since there'd been so much as a single whisper
about him. These days, she suspected he was a reformed
character, very much like herself.

Not that it mattered. Even if she'd believed the whispers,
or believed in magic, even if Rousseau weren't, by all
accounts, happily married, the new Sophie would still have
to think long and hard before she gambled what was left of
her uncertain future on voodoo. Who knew what kind of
price you'd have to pay for something like that?

The old Sophie wouldn't have cared about any of that.
Then again, the old Sophie would have been eating breakfast
inside the café. She'd have done Rousseau in a heartbeat —
probably right there on the counter — without thinking twice
about the voodoo *or* the happily married.

The old Sophie had been kind of a bitch, now that she thought about it.

Not that one, cher, a soft voice seemed to whisper in her ear. *He's not for you.*

Sophie heaved a sigh. *Yeah, yeah. Tell me something I don't already know.* Not that one and not any other one either, as far as she could see. That was okay. She was used to it by now. She'd made her peace with the idea that she'd likely be spending the rest of her life alone at about the same time she opted against having her breasts reconstructed.

If she'd only lost one, things might have been different. She might have had a reason then to go through more surgery and another lengthy recovery in order to build a new breast that would kind-of-sort-of- no-not-really match her existing one. But to put herself through all that torture just to set herself up with an *entirely* fake rack? Two featureless mounds that would never look right or feel authentic and that would only serve as a constant reminder of what she'd lost? Yeah, that was so not happening.

How on earth was tacking two alien appendages onto her already ravaged body supposed to help her overcome her new aversion to viewing herself naked? There was only one thing they'd be good for—helping her to attract new lovers into her bed. Lovers who, in all likelihood, would be gone in a flash anyway, once they'd figured things out.

Seriously, who needed that?

She might as well spare everyone the disappointment in store for them by letting them know up front exactly what they were getting—or not getting—where her body was concerned. If they couldn't accept her as she was, did she really want them anyway?

Brave words. Do you really mean them?

Yes, damn it, she did. Much as she mourned what she'd lost, if she'd had it to do over again, if she were to be presented once more with the exact same set of shitty-assed circumstances, she was pretty sure she'd make the very same choices.

Life was more than just her breasts. *She* was more than just her breasts. If she had to sacrifice a part to safeguard the whole, so be it. As long as she could open her eyes every morning and continue to put one foot in front of another all day, as long as she could stay healthy, stay cancer free, stay alive, she intended to at least try to enjoy the moments she was given and live each one to the fullest. She might not be raking in as many beads as before at Mardi Gras, and her steadiest beau might always be the one who lived in the drawer of her bedside table, but on the plus side, she was saving one helluva lot on sports bras.

Sophie started as a passerby stumbling along the banquette suddenly lost his footing and slammed into her table. She grabbed for her coffee to keep it from spilling when the wrought iron table tilted precariously under the man's unsteady weight.

"Watch out!" Glancing up, she found herself staring into the bleary blue eyes of a drunken, storefront Santa. Well, that was life in the Quarter for you, she supposed as her heart continued its attempts to beat itself right out of her chest. The smell of whisky and peppermint schnapps wafting off the man was so strong it made her head spin. She pressed her free hand to her chest, willing her heart to slow the fuck down.

Santa blinked back at her, still resting his weight on the tabletop, a crumpled piece of paper clutched in one fist. A slow smile curved his lips. Eyes twinkling, he leaned in closer and leered.

"Well, hey there, boo.Where y'at? You bein' naughty or nice?"

Before Sophie could even fashion a reply, Rousseau appeared in the doorway. He scowled menacingly at the man. "Get out of here. Quit harassing my customer."

Santa straightened up, his expression one of affronted dignity as he glared at Rousseau. "Ain't harassin' no one. She tripped me."

"I did no such thing," Sophie spluttered. She flashed the man an indignant look, then watched in relief as he lurched stiffly away. A flicker of motion from her tabletop caught her eye. The badly creased paper Santa had left behind fluttered weakly in the slight breeze. "Hey, wait!" she said as she snatched it up, intending to return it. Then she took a closer look.

Midnight Ink. New Beginnings Special.
Discounted rates for survivor and memorial ink.
Are you ready for a new beginning? Say it in ink.
Call, or visit us online for more information...

It's a sign, that same soft voice insisted.

Oh, it was a sign all right. Sophie bit back a sigh. Hearing voices was a *definite* sign that she was losing her mind. Still, she couldn't help but appreciate the irony. It wasn't as if New Orleans was hurting for tattoo shops, so what were the odds she'd be handed a flyer for the very shop where she'd gone for her own tattoos? Come to think of it, maybe it *was* a sign after all.

"What you got there?" Rousseau asked as he ambled closer. He tilted his head to read the flyer. "Are you thinking of getting another tattoo?"

Was she? She already had several, but she hadn't added anything to her "collection" in several years. "Oh, I don't know." But even as she said it, an image flashed through her mind of a picture she'd recently seen online. It had shown a woman's heavily tattooed torso, flowers and elaborate scrollwork covering over the scars from her mastectomies.

That tattoo hadn't really been Sophie's style, but the idea of once again being able to celebrate her body, of enjoying it, flaws and all, of showing it off rather than always feeling the need to hide it away beneath layers of clothing, that had appealed to her. A lot. She wasn't even sure if it was possible for her to feel that way about herself ever again, but if it was, if there was any chance at all...

Sophie felt a thrill of excitement as the idea took hold. A new beginning, huh? Well, why the fuck not? "You know what?" Smiling, she unzipped her jacket pocket to get to her phone. "I think maybe I am."

Sophie dialed the number quickly before she could chicken out and change her mind. It was before noon, so she wasn't even sure the shop would be open yet, but the phone was picked up on the second ring.

"Midnight Ink." The lilting voice on the phone was female; she sounded young and perky, carefree — everything Sophie wasn't. Sophie's heart lurched. Shit was about to get real.

"Hi. I'm, uh...I'm calling about your new beginnings special." Sophie fingered the flyer in her hand. "I...I had surgery a couple of years ago for breast cancer, and I'm interested in getting a chest piece done. You know, to cover the scars? Would that qualify for your special rates?"

"Yes, of course," the voice replied, no longer quite so perky. "Um...let me see where I can fit you in, okay? Did you have a particular artist in mind? Or a particular time frame that was better for you?"

"No. Not really. I mean, I just saw your flyer and...I haven't actually had time to think about it all that much." Sign or no sign, Sophie suddenly found herself wondering if getting a new tattoo was such a stellar idea after all. Memories of the last time she'd gotten inked flashed through her mind bringing heat and longing and even more uncertainty.

Declan's voice teasing her through the worst of it; his hands, firm yet gentle on her flesh, reassuring; the expression on his face, focused, patient, intent...

Sometimes a tattoo was *not* just a tattoo; it was personal, almost too personal to trust to a stranger. At the moment, it seemed that her exhibitionist streak had gone the way of her breasts. Could she really go through with this? Did she really want to bare her chest to a stranger when she could hardly stand to look in the mirror at herself? Maybe she could ask about a female artist? Maybe that would help. Or maybe she should just forget the whole idea. "Maybe I should think about it some more."

"Hmm. Okay, well, actually, it looks like all our regular artists are pretty booked up right now," the voice on the phone told her.

Sophie exhaled. Her shoulders sagged—relief, mixed with just a trace of disappointment. "Oh. All right. Well, thanks anyway for checking. I guess it's not meant to be. Maybe another time then."

"Whoa, hold on there. Not so fast. I wasn't done yet. I'm *sure* we can squeeze you in somewhere. You know, we're also making appointments for our guest artist, Declan Ross. He'll be tattooing here for a few weeks. Is there any chance you'd be interested in working with him?"

"Declan's back?" Talk about signs! This one was billboard-sized and covered in day-glo neon. "Isn't he...I mean, I guess I thought he was still out on the West Coast."

"Oh, yeah. Well, I mean, he's not here *yet*. Like I said, he's coming in primarily for the fundraiser at the end of the month. So...I take it you're interested then?"

Having Declan here—that was a game changer. If he was the one tattooing her, it would be just like old times. And the chance to see him again... That alone could make it all worthwhile. Maybe she *could* do this after all. "Yes. Yes, I think I am."

"Well, good! Why don't you go ahead and give me your information, and we'll get you signed up."

"Yeah, okay. Sure," Sophie answered, barely aware of what she was saying. Declan was coming back. It was the last thing she'd been expecting. And, now, in just a few weeks she'd be seeing him again.

Now, that one you can have, cher. This time, Sophie would swear the voice laughed out loud. *That one's all yours. He's got your name written all over him.*

Chapter Two

He's got your name written all over him...

That damn voice was still cackling excitedly in Sophie's head when she returned to her apartment later that day, and frankly, she was sick of it. She and Declan had been a lot of things to each other. They'd been friends, playmates, lovers, confidants; they'd had each other's backs easily a dozen times. But if there was one thing Declan Ross had never been, nor ever would be, it was *all hers*. Or all anyone's really.

The boy had issues—big and apparently insurmountable. As a result, he'd forgotten how to love...anyone really. It was sad but true, and she'd long since resigned herself to the fact. Most people probably assumed it was nothing more than a simple fear of intimacy or commitment, but Sophie knew it was bigger than that.

Had she ever wished things could be different? Of course she had. She'd been half in love with him for years and completely in lust with him for even longer than that. But, then again, who hadn't been?

It was odd really. He was good-looking, but not stunningly so, and not nearly as tall in real life as pictures and television made him seem. He was a good friend and a good artist but as a human being, he definitely had his faults. He was honest and direct, but not particularly sensitive. The subtle gene had totally passed him by. If you asked his opinion on something, you'd best be looking for the unvarnished truth. On the other hand, when it suited him, he could charm the pants off of practically anyone.

Ever since his debut on the popular series *Inked in O-Town*, he'd been making a career of acting like a jackass on national TV. Frankly, she'd never thought it seemed like that much of a stretch. Yet people loved him anyway.

All the personal charisma that made him so popular on TV was even more potent in real life. Even back when he was just starting out, Sophie was pretty sure he could have bedded at least nine-tenths of the women he tattooed if he'd wanted to. For all she knew, he had. She'd given up worrying about *that* the day she realized she was only going to make herself crazy. She was never going to be able to fix what was wrong with Declan, and he was unlikely to change on his own. The best she could do was to be his friend, enjoy the ride, and keep her own feelings in check.

It wasn't even his fault that he was the way he was. Some wounds simply ran too deep to heal; they just scarred over. As long as he was content to remain emotionally unavailable, to remain mired in the past—in his own guilt and pain and heartbreak—it was hopeless. She doubted he'd ever be able to move forward. And, unless he did, no good was ever going to come from losing her heart to him.

Sophie opened the door to her apartment and was immediately greeted by her roommate's cat. She'd been caring for Lagniappe while Lida was out of town. The big, gray tomcat rubbed against her ankles, meowing loudly to get her attention. He weaved between her legs, his tail quivering with anticipation, seemingly unaware that his actions were hampering her efforts to get to the kitchen where his food was stored. It was a miracle she didn't trip over him.

Lida always claimed that his extra toes—the *little something extra* for which he was named—made him especially sure-footed. If that was true, Sophie wished she'd been born polydactyl herself. He was a handsome cat, yes, but definitely not worth falling and breaking an arm for.

Handsome, affectionate, totally focused on his own needs and completely oblivious to how easily he could hurt her... Hmm. Didn't that sound familiar? It was probably just because he was already on her mind, but at the moment, Lagniappe reminded Sophie an awful lot of Declan.

After she'd fed the cat and poured herself a glass of sweet tea, Sophie collected her sketchpad and a set of watercolor pencils and took a seat on the couch. All day she'd been brainstorming ideas for her tattoo. Oriental poppies were currently at the top of her list, in part because they were her birth month flower. Their bold shapes and bright colors struck her as being cheerful and dramatic, exactly the kind of thing that couldn't help but lift her spirits whenever she looked at them. Or so she hoped.

She'd switched on the television before she sat down — mostly because she liked the noise. It kept her company while she worked. After only a few minutes, however, she found herself putting the sketchpad aside and reaching for the remote once again. She couldn't help herself.

She scrolled through the list of shows she'd recorded earlier until she found the one she wanted, then pressed play on a recent episode of *Inked in O-Town*. It was one she'd seen before and, yes, Declan was heavily featured, but that's not entirely why she chose it.

Declan's client in this episode was a serviceman who'd been injured in an explosion. Sophie could tell herself she'd chosen it because she wanted to study Declan's technique, because she wanted to watch his face while he covered up scars that were, in some ways, even worse than her own, or because she needed to convince herself that this was something they could both handle.

All that was true, but there was a much more basic reason too. She might hate herself for being so weak, but sometimes she just got hungry for the sight of his face.

Of course, the years had brought a few changes to that face she missed. The scruffy beard and longish hair had been early casualties. They'd been replaced the very first season by a shorter, more stylish cut and a meticulously groomed goatee. One thing that hadn't changed was his voice. One of her favorite things about watching him on TV was that she also got to listen to him. She got to listen to him *a lot*. Because it seemed like he rarely ever shut up.

He'd always been vocal — especially in bed. It wasn't just dirty talk either, although he'd certainly excelled at that. He'd made demands, made promises, made observations; more than anything, it seemed, he'd used words to direct their lovemaking. And Sophie had loved it when he did.

It had been kind of an eye-opener. She was not the world's most passive person, either in bed or out. Following orders was not her thing. Being restrained, being told what to do, begging to come, begging for pain — hell, begging for anything — she'd never had any degree of interest in any of it, until she got around Declan, and then she couldn't get enough.

Something about him made her crave it. Even now, even just the sound of his voice on TV, when he was talking to someone else in a totally non-sexual context, caused her whole body to flush with heat.

"Stretch your arm above your head," Declan said. "And let me get this stencil in place over your ribcage. Yeah, that's nice. This is gonna be a good one."

Sophie abandoned all pretense of working. She slid lower on the couch and slipped her hand into her pants, imagining it was Declan's, calling up the memory of one of the last times she'd seen him...

It was after he'd gotten the call about the show. They'd gone out to celebrate and then come back to the tiny studio where she'd been living. They were in the hallway, outside her door, and she'd just turned her key in the lock when he stopped her. He took her by the shoulders and turned her around to face him.

She wasn't surprised when he kissed her or when the kiss lingered on and on. It had hit her too that evening. The clock was ticking. Things were changing between them. He was leaving soon, and the odds weren't good that they'd have many more nights like tonight. What did surprise her was when she felt him pop the button on her jeans and lower the zipper.

"What are you doing?" she asked against his lips when he slipped his hand into her pants, one long finger stroking over her clit. She shuddered in response, barely resisting the urge to buck against his hand. "Stop...oh, God that feels good."

"Gonna make you come," he muttered, his voice husky and raw.

She didn't doubt it. And, on the whole, she was heavily in favor of the idea. There was just one small problem. "Wait. Let's get inside first."

"No. Here."

"That's uh...that's a really bad idea." They'd both had a few drinks, but she wouldn't have said either of them was drunk. So why was he acting this way? "C'mon, stop. Someone might see."

"Yeah. Want 'em to." The hand that wasn't in her pants clenched in her hair. He tugged her head back and nipped at her throat, and her mind went blank. "Want everyone to know."

Sophie whimpered in response. "Know what?"

"What you do to me."

Okay, that was… "Backwards. Totally ass-backwards." All anyone was going to see was what he did to her — which was to make her lose her ever-loving mind.

Declan sucked harder on her neck, an evil chuckle vibrating in his chest. "Okay, if that's what you want. We could do that. I could take you from behind right here."

"What? No!"

"Why not? Isn't that what you just said? You'd like it too. I know you would."

"I would not. I…I…I…" Oh, fuck. Yes, she would too. Her nipples got so hard at the thought it felt as though they were going to burn right through her shirt. She wanted him to turn her around, press her hard against the door. What was wrong with her?

"Mmm. Wet," Declan murmured as his fingers continued to play with her pussy. "I might have to strip off these jeans right here and have a taste."

In another minute, she'd probably let him. Sophie groaned. It was time for drastic action. She fumbled around behind her back until she located the doorknob. She grabbed it and turned. The door, propelled by their joint weight pressing against it, swung open. Her hand on the doorknob helped her stay upright, the door itself supporting her. Declan, on the other hand, completely lost his balance. He stumbled forward several steps before tripping and landing on the floor. Sophie couldn't help but laugh at his pained expression as he lay groaning on the tile.

He twisted around and looked at her. "Laughing? Oh, hell no. You're so gonna pay for that."

Declan climbed to his feet, eyes gleaming with mischief. Sophie dodged around him as he reached for her and ran — making it all the way across the room before he caught her. She thought she knew what was coming next. Thought she'd be over his lap in the next minute with her jeans pulled down just enough for him to lay his hand on her cheeks.

That first slap landing on her ass always sounded so loud—horrifyingly so. A wave of heat would wash up her face until even her ears burned. She'd be mortified, embarrassed and completely turned on. She'd be convinced the whole building could hear it, that the whole block knew exactly what he was doing to her, and how much she loved it. By the time the third slap struck home her eyes would be watering from the sting. By the fifth, she'd no longer hear the sound his hand made as it struck her heated flesh—in part due to the rush of blood in her ears, in part because, by then, her moans would have drowned out any other sounds. If they made it to ten, she'd cream so hard she'd leave wet patches on his pants.

He'd pretend annoyance and order her to her knees, instructing her to suck him off good for her penance. She loved that even more. She loved tracing the veins along his shaft with her tongue. Loved teasing the ridge with her tongue piercing. Loved tasting his cum. Filling her mouth with him. Losing her breath on each deep downstroke. His hand in her hair exerting just the right amount of pressure really sent her over the top.

Her heels folded beneath her would draw her attention to her sore ass. Pressure would build between her thighs, the need to come. She'd try to clamp her legs together in an effort to alleviate it. If he let her. He rarely did. Usually, he'd demand she keep them spread so he could watch. Usually, she'd be naked, and he'd toy with her nipples as well, tugging and twisting the little gold bars of her piercings until she'd completely lost her mind.

The harder I pull, the better you suck, he'd always tell her. And if he hadn't restrained her arms, if he'd left her hands free so she could play with herself, she wouldn't need anything more than that. His voice, those words, and she'd be coming to pieces right there on the floor with his cock in her mouth.

This time, he surprised her. He tumbled her onto the bed, rolling with her until she was pinned beneath him with only one arm free.

He smiled down at her. "Now, where was I?" Since his hand had reclaimed its place in her hair, and was already exerting that delicious pressure she'd come to crave, Sophie was pretty sure they both knew exactly where they were— and where they were going.

All the same, a little reminder never hurt. She gazed up at him expectantly. "I believe you said something about making me come?"

"Hmm. We'll see about that. Stretch your arm up over your head and leave it there."

"Like this?" she asked as she moved her arm into position.

"Perfect." He pushed her shirt and bra out of the way. "Now don't move again until I tell you."

"I'm not sure I can do that." Much as she wanted his touch, the idea of not being able to shield herself if she wanted to unnerved her.

"Am I going to have to tie you up?"

Sophie gasped in surprise, not because it would be the first time they'd done it, but because she'd only just now remembered a key point about the last time they'd done it here. Afterward, she'd never actually gotten around to removing the padded handcuffs they'd affixed to the bed frame.

Declan had obviously learned to read her expression with uncanny accuracy. Either that or he'd read her mind. His gaze turned speculative as he stretched his own arm toward the corner of the bed. He rooted around for a moment in the space between the bed frame and the wall. "Aha." His eyes were sparkling when his hand re-emerged holding the slightly dusty, cream-colored cuff.

Sophie bit her lip. Her heart was pounding. Her thoughts tumbled over one another in her mind. *Yes. No. Yes!*

"Trust me?"

She had to clear her throat before she could answer. "Yes."

"Sure about that?"

She was. She wanted that thrill of vulnerability, even if it was mostly make-believe. In a weird way, it made her feel closer to him somehow, as though she'd let him inside her skin. When he restrained her like this, even a little bit, the outside world seemed to fade away. Her focus shrank and sharpened until it seemed like nothing even existed anymore except the two of them. She licked her lips, wanting desperately to explain even part of that—how close she felt to him tonight, how very much she'd miss him—but she was out of words. She met his gaze and nodded, hoping he'd read a little of *that* in her eyes as well, and then barely managed not to flinch when he snugged the cuff in place a little more tightly than usual.

Shivers raced across her skin as his hand stroked down her arm, his gaze never leaving her face. He briefly cupped one breast, chaffing the sensitive tip with the pad of his thumb, but then moved on to slip his hand into her pants once again.

She bucked a little against him. "Jeans. Off."

But Declan shook his head. "Uh-uh. I've changed my mind about that. I want you like this. I don't even want you to move. I want to see if I can make you come using nothing but my hand and the sound of my voice."

Sophie groaned impatiently. Well, of course he could do that! Hadn't he already proven it a thousand times over? She was pretty sure he could make her come using just his voice alone if they wanted to devote the entire night to the task.

Tension ratcheted tighter. Having been told she couldn't, Sophie wanted to move even more than usual. She wanted to arch and squirm and grind against Declan's hand. Her pussy pulsed and ached with need. Exquisite though the sensations were, she needed more. "Bite me," she whispered when she could take no more. "Hard."

He met her gaze. "What?"

Heat flared in her cheeks. This was new — and a little bit edgy, even for them. She couldn't repeat it. "Please."

Declan groaned softly. His hand tightened in her hair. Sophie's heart beat faster as anticipation further sharpened her need. She squeezed her eyes shut.

"Open your eyes, *bébé*," Declan whispered as his lips grazed hers.

It was a struggle to comply. Her heavy-lidded eyes didn't want to stay open.

Holding her gaze, Declan lowered his mouth to her breast. He teased the tip with his tongue, tugged on the piercing until Sophie was whimpering with need, and all the while his hand stayed busy between her legs He circled her clit with a firm, steady touch while the tips of two fingers pumped inside her. It was barely deep enough to count as penetration, but it provided exactly enough friction, exactly in that spot where her flesh was already over-sensitized.

Sophie gulped for breath. Her nerves were on overload. When Declan's teeth finally closed on her breast, sharper than ever before, hard enough to leave marks, she flew apart. Declan held her through the aftershocks, gently cupping her mound, whispering soft words in her ear ...

Back in the present, all alone on her couch, Sophie shuddered through another orgasm. Declan's voice was still there to soothe her.

She refocused her gaze on the television, where Declan was hard at work. Even filtered through the lens of a camera, it was impossible not to see or be impressed by the passion he brought to his work. Maybe that was the real secret to his success?

Soon, she was the one he'd have on his table, the focus of all his attention. His hands on her flesh, his gaze making love to her skin, leaving marks. Leaving more marks. As though he hadn't marked her enough already.

After she'd come that night five years ago, after he'd released her wrist, stripped off her jeans, and fucked her almost senseless, they'd lain together in bed. He'd been in a jubilant mood, full of plans for the future. It took him several minutes to even notice she was crying.

"What's wrong?" he asked. It was probably petty of her to be annoyed by the fact that he sounded more puzzled by her tears than truly concerned.

She shrugged. "Nothing really. I know it's stupid, but it just hit me how much I'm going to miss you." It was true, but only half the story. What she'd also realized was how abysmally unsuccessful she'd been at restraining her emotions. It was actually a *good* thing he was leaving. A very good thing. It would save her the humiliation of having to admit to her deeper feelings. Or, even worse, begging him to love her back.

Declan squeezed her tight. "So what's the problem? You'll come visit, right? Besides, who knows if things will even work out with the show? I could be back by Christmas. Probably you won't even have time to miss me."

Sophie nodded, smiling through her tears, playing along. "Hmm. There is that. Given your track record, I guess it would be kind of a miracle if you managed to keep *this* job for more than a few weeks, huh?" But it was bullshit and she was pretty sure they both knew it. He would *not* be back by Christmas, no matter what happened with the show; he would probably not be coming back at all. Sure his roots were in New Orleans, going back for several generations, but the past few years had seen those roots ripped out and stomped on hard. That was probably not the kind of thing from which you could ever recover. He'd been barely hanging on, slowly dying in place — they both knew that too.

Once he got away from here, once he started a new life somewhere else, why would he ever turn back? He'd put down new roots. Deeper, stronger, healthier than ever before. If she were a true friend, why wouldn't she want that for him? Why wouldn't she want him to grow and thrive, even if that meant she'd likely never see him again? It certainly wouldn't surprise her if he chose to cut all ties to his former life — herself included — and if she were smart, she'd do the same. One quick, preemptive incision. Because the cleaner the cut, the easier it would heal.

Five years down the road, she could see that she'd been right. Hopefully, by now, enough time had passed that they could see each other again, take pleasure in what they'd once had, maybe even indulge in a little harmless nostalgia, without any danger of either of them backsliding.

At the very least, she hoped she could look forward to seeing Declan secure in the knowledge that her feelings were once again under control. She was over him.

Chapter Three

Three weeks later…

"Okay. You're all set." Declan smoothed a final piece of tape into place, securing a layer of plastic wrap over the tattoo he'd just finished — his last of the day.

The pretty blonde who was his latest client slowly sat up on the padded table, her T-shirt clasped against her chest. "Thank you," she said as she gingerly slipped the shirt over her head and then tugged her clothes back into place. "It's beautiful."

Declan nodded. "I told you it would be." He'd designed the tattoo — an abstract, deconstructed peacock — to follow the lines of her body. It flowed along her curves, from shoulder to hip, in a sinuous cascade of perfect, paisley-shaped feathers. "I'm glad you like it."

It bore only the slightest resemblance to the tattoo she'd thought she was getting when she'd come in today — and a damn good thing too. The pictures she'd sent in as examples of what she was looking to get had been boring and uninteresting and didn't really work with his style. They were too simple, too small, and would have required entirely too much line work. Plus, she wanted it across her lower back, which was totally the wrong placement for something like this.

Declan took his craft seriously. The watercolor-style tattoos for which he was becoming well known always looked better on a larger canvas. It hadn't taken much to convince her of that and to make her see the wisdom of letting him give her what *he* wanted.

Plenty of artists would have been all too happy to give her just another, generic-looking tattoo, but she'd come to *him*. It would be nice to think she'd come for his eye, his talent, his artistry, for all the experience he brought to the table. In all likelihood, however, what she'd come for the Declan Ross she thought she knew from TV.

Luckily for him, *that* Declan didn't do run-of-the-mill ho tags either.

"Now be sure and read over this sheet," Declan instructed as he handed her the page he'd had printed detailing his personal aftercare suggestions. "It's got a lot of important information. You'll want to keep it covered for the first couple of hours, but that's all. After that, you'll want to rinse it off, pat it dry and leave it uncovered as much as possible while it's healing. You'll also want to stop on your way home and pick up some calendula cream. I know you'll hear otherwise, but trust me; you really want to steer clear of petroleum-based products, scented-lotions and especially sunscreen."

"Calendula cream," she repeated dutifully, as though she had no idea what he was talking about. She probably didn't.

"Or coconut oil. That's good too, but I don't know if you can find organic around here. If not, you're really better off sticking with the calendula."

"Okay." She nodded for a moment, still seated on the edge of the table, gazing at him expectantly, making no move to leave.

Declan clapped his hands together. "Okay. Good. So. Any last questions for me?"

"Yes." Immediately, she thrust the paper back at him. "Can I get your autograph?"

Declan pretended not to notice the rolled eyes, the faked coughs, the snorts of derisive laughter the other artists tried to muffle. Bastards. They were just jealous because no one was asking for theirs. "Sure thing," he said as he forced a smile. He grabbed a marker off the closest counter and then paused. "Who should I make it out to?"

"Oh, it's for me."

Declan waited.

"Make it out to Chrissy."

"Chrissy. Right." He hurriedly scrawled his name, added a couple of platitudes, and then handed the paper back to her. "But, seriously, Chrissy, I need you to follow the instructions on this. All right? They're important." It really annoyed him when clients failed to care for their tattoos. He did good work, but once someone left his chair, he had no control over what happened. He hated when a good tat got messed up because some dumbass didn't follow directions. "C'mon." He held out his hand to help the girl down from the table. "Let me walk you out."

He hadn't taken more than a few steps before Shep Montgomery looked up from the sleeve he was working on and called out to him, "Hey, Ross."

"Yeah?" Declan turned his head and warily eyed his former mentor. It's not like he wasn't used to it by now, but it was rarely a good sign when someone addressed him by his last name.

"I don't know what you've gotten used to out there in Hollywood, but around here, we still have to clean up after ourselves."

"Really?" The words were out before Declan could stop himself. "'Cause that's not how I remember it."

He cast an involuntary glance around the shop, taking it all in; the brick walls, the stainless steel, the sinks, the counters, the padded black vinyl, the red and black paint, the gaudy gold trim. He loved tattoo shops. He loved everything about them—the smells, the sounds, the artwork on the walls, the funky, edgy vibe they invariably gave off. But he did not especially love cleaning them. And, the way he recalled it, back when he'd first come to work at Midnight Ink—back when the legendary Henry Lee Cairn still owned the shop and Declan was just a fiery-eyed, tattoo artist wannabe and Shep's lowly apprentice—that's mostly what he'd done.

Even after he'd progressed to the point where he was allowed to set up his own station and tattoo on his own, without supervision, as low man on the totem pole, he'd still had to clean up after himself *and* everyone else. Not to mention cover for the receptionist on her days off. Good times—not.

One thing he had absolutely *not* come back to New Orleans to do was to pick up where he'd left off. He was here to help publicize a good cause. One of the charities that would benefit from the New Year's Eve tattoo-a-palooza was his own pet cause, the Wounded Warriors Project. His father had been in the military. He'd come back from the first Gulf War with PTSD and killed himself when Declan was just a kid. Whatever Declan could do to help other kids from having to go through what he'd gone through, he'd do it. No questions. Not even when it meant having to put up with a certain amount of crap from his co-workers. His *former* co-workers.

"Anyway, it's Oakland, all right? Not Hollywood. And relax. I'm not gone for the day. I'll take care of it before I leave."

Shep nodded. "A'ight. See that you do. And don't leave it too long either."

On the other hand, there was a limit to *how much* crap Declan was willing to take. "Oh, yes, sir, Mr. Montgomery. I will jump on that *right* away." He flipped him off with a muttered, "And *you* can jump on *this*."

An excited giggle at his shoulder recalled Declan's attention.

Chrissy looked fascinated. No. Worse. She looked freaking turned on. So *this* was what she'd come here for, bratty Declan, the artist everyone loved to hate — especially the other artists. Fan-fucking-tastic. He could just imagine her hauling out her cell phone the minute she hit the banquette, getting her girlfriends on the line so she could tell them all how, *it was so awesome! Omigod, you guys, it was just like being on an episode of* Inked in O-Town!

All the thoughts he'd been entertaining while he'd tattooed her, of asking her if she wanted to meet up with him later for a drink, of inviting her back to his hotel room after that, were forgotten. There was no way he was tapping that.

Still, as his agent never tired of reminding him, giving the audience what they wanted was as big a part of his job now as the actual tattoos. So he flashed her a wink and his trademark smirk, then guided her as quickly as possible toward the front of the shop. Celebrity Declan would just have to suck it up; he'd have to live with not getting laid for one more night.

He supposed he shouldn't really resent all the crap that came along with his success. He'd known what he was letting himself in for when he signed on to play a jerkified version of himself on television. Or, as his last girlfriend had preferred to put it, someone who was *maybe just a little bit more* of a jerk on camera than he was in real life. But who cared what she thought? He made good money doing what he did and she sure hadn't complained when he was spending most of it on her.

Last he heard, Tonya had moved to LA and was dating some kind of football player. So how much sensitivity and self-awareness could she really have been looking for in a guy anyway?

As long as it continued to bring in the Benjamins, he guessed he'd just keep playing himself for as many seasons as they'd let him. Being loud, rude, and obnoxious sure hadn't hurt his reputation as an artist any—or his bank account, for that matter. These days, he was busier than he'd ever been.

The small waiting area at the front of the shop was mostly empty. A couple of people sat around, paging idly through the various ink magazines or artists' portfolios stacked on the coffee table. They didn't even look up when he passed through the room—and, man, wasn't that a relief?

Sassy, the shop's current receptionist, was busy at her computer, bangles jingling as she typed. After seeing his client out, Declan went over and leaned on the front counter, waiting patiently for her to finish what she was doing. The streak in her hair was red today. Shiny and festive, it glowed with an almost metallic sheen. What was it with the women who worked here and their multi-hued hair? He wondered if they purposely planned for it to complement their tattoos. Come to think of it, maybe Sassy and Roisin coordinated those with each other as well, so as not to clash. It wasn't impossible. They looked damned good together. In fact, he'd love to paint a portrait of the two of them. It would have to be nude, or semi-nude, but he was pretty sure he could talk them into that. He was good at talking women into things.

He'd pose them right there on the couch, with Sassy draped languidly across Roisin's lap, sleek and contented as a cat. Her rich, caramel-and-chocolate coloring would be a perfect foil for Roisin's cool porcelain skin and raven hair. Roisin's blue eyes would stare challengingly out of the canvas, straight at the viewer, straight at him, as she raked her fingers through Sassy's hair, or dipped her hand lower to palm the other girl's breast...

"Earth to Declan." Sassy's voice snapped him back to the present. "Did you need something?"

"Uh, yeah. Sorry." Declan pasted on his most winning smile. "My mind must've wandered."

"Uh-huh. So I'd assumed. And I guess your eyes went right along for the ride, huh? Maybe you wanna lock those puppies up from now on, okay? Now, what can I do for you?"

"Well, here's the thing. I'd really love a cup of coffee right about now, but I think Shep's gonna have my balls if I try and sneak out to get some before I clean up my station. You wouldn't happen to know of a good place around here that delivers, would you?"

Sassy's eyes narrowed. "Are you telling me that coffee pot is empty *again?*"

Coffee pot? "I, uh..."

"No." Gold bangles slid up her arm in a jangling rush as Sassy held up a hand to stop him. "I don't know why I even ask. Of course it's empty. Never mind. I'll deal with it. Meanwhile *you* are running late." She picked up a sheaf of papers and slapped them down on the counter. "Your next client's been waiting on you. I didn't realize your last session was going to run so long. Your station's just gonna have to wait. Hopefully your balls will survive."

"My next what?" It was Declan's turn to frown. "Oh, hell no. Are you kidding me? I am *not* doing back-to-back tattoos today. What is this, paint-by-numbers? Just because I made an exception for tomorrow's New Year's Eve party, doesn't mean I plan on doing it all the time."

"And are you through being a diva now? It's not a tat, okay? So chillax. It's just a consult, one which *you* requested, by the way. So I'm sure you can handle it even without the caffeine fix. I don't know what you're freaking out about. I sent you the artwork *weeks* ago, along with your schedule. Didn't you even look at it?"

His schedule—right. The one he'd ignored while he'd been working round-the-clock to free-up time in his calendar for this trip. The one he'd barely glanced at during his flight here because, by that point, he was too exhausted to think. "Sure I did."

"Seriously?"

"Yeah. A little." Still frowning, Declan picked up the papers and rifled through them. "Oh. *This* one." An unwilling smile crossed his face. "Yeah, I remember now." This was the one tattoo he was really looking forward to. It was just his style. The pictures that had been sent as guidelines were perfect, a series of delicate watercolor paintings of poppies, from full blown to just unfurling, to tightly budded, their details picked out in pen and ink. Bold yet feminine, quirky and just abstract enough to be interesting, the only thing he wasn't sure about yet was how he was going to bend the images to fit the contours of a woman's body, without distorting them beyond recognition. Which is why he'd insisted on meeting with the client ahead of time.

He'd already done some preliminary stencils using some of the individual flowers as guides, but that was about as far as he could go without having a better idea of the body he was attempting to fit them to. Or maybe he could change his unknown client's mind. Get her to make it a back piece instead. Or let him wrap an entire leg in giant poppies. How hard could it be? "Sorry. I didn't realize this was what was on the schedule for tonight. It's not a problem. I *love* this one."

"Don't waste time telling *me* that, sugar." Sassy nodded at the room behind him. "Tell *her*."

Her? Who, her? Declan glanced at the release form in his hand, quickly searching for a name. When he found it, he froze. "No way." He turned away from the counter, his eyes searching for her face. "Sophie Jane. I don't believe it."

"Hey, Declan. Long time, huh?" Sophie's voice was exactly as he remembered it. Her smile, on the other hand, was far more cautious. Her face was pale, her arms were folded almost defensively across her chest, and her eyes held a sadness that tugged at his heart.

"C'mere, you," he said as he pulled her in for a hug that could have set new records for extreme awkwardness.

It started out okay. The smell of her hair and her skin was so familiar, so right; it felt like coming home. For just an instant, when she rested her head on his shoulder, relaxing against him like she always used to do, he could almost imagine he'd never left.

"Welcome home," she whispered. But the words sounded hollow and she didn't hug him back.

Her arms had been crossed when he'd grabbed her. He'd assumed she'd unclasp them and wrap them around his waist, but instead they'd gotten twisted up between them. When he squeezed her tight, all he could feel were bones and hard angles, rather than the softness he'd remembered and longed to feel again. It was obvious she'd lost weight. She was disturbingly thin, blow-away-in-a-stiff-breeze skinny from the feel of her. All too soon she was pulling away.

As Declan's gaze slid over her body he felt himself frown. Had it really been only five years since he'd seen her? Looking at her now, it felt so much longer. Her beautiful hair had all been hacked off, and what in the hell was she wearing?

The old Sophie had never met a bandage dress she didn't fall instantly in love with. The shorter and tighter it was, the better she liked it. She hadn't been afraid to show off her curves or more than a little skin. She'd loved low-cut tops, painted-on jeans, anything that bared her midriff, and she'd proudly rocked some of the tallest, spikiest fuck-me heels he'd ever seen. She'd been game for anything, and the way she dressed made sure everyone knew it.

Today's Sophie, on the other hand, came wrapped in a billowy poet's shirt, buttoned to the neck and topped by a long, filmy scarf that fell in loops across her chest. Sure, her skirt was short and her boots were high, but between the shirt and the scarf and the tense, defensive posture, it was as though she'd become a different person since he'd seen her last.

"So what's with the outfit?" Declan asked, flicking at the scarf. "And, Jesus Christ, girl, your hair!"

Sophie's cheeks turned pink. She fingered the ends of her pixie-short cut and laughed nervously. "Oh. Yeah. That…"

"I cannot believe you cut it."

"Well, I kinda had to."

"Honest to God, Declan," Sassy growled. "Where are your fucking *manners?*" Her cheeks were as flushed as Sophie's and the expression on her face was one of mortified disbelief.

Declan's eyebrows rose. "What? Was that rude? We're friends, all right? Friends are allowed to say things like that to each other." He turned back to Sophie because it was her opinion that mattered after all. "Aren't they?"

Sophie rolled her eyes. "Same old Declan," she said with something like her old spirit. Sassy just shook her head.

Always, in the past, Declan had felt as though he could tell Sophie anything, confide secrets he wouldn't dream of mentioning to anyone else. The idea that maybe things had changed, that he couldn't do that now, disappointed him almost as much as the sight of her super-short hair—and that he *still* could not believe.

Her hair had been fucking gorgeous long—soft, thick, goddess-quality, honey-gold waves. She *knew* how much he'd always loved it, so she couldn't possibly be surprised by his reaction. He had vivid memories of just how it had felt to have those silky strands wrapped around his fist—far more vivid than they should be for being a good five years old, and even despite the fact that he'd jerked off to her image in his mind more times over the years than he cared to count.

For all that she'd complained about New Orleans heat and threatened to cut her hair short at least ten times every summer, he'd never imagined she'd actually go through with it. She'd liked it too much when he tugged on it— especially when he was bending her over and taking her from behind or if she was on her knees sucking him off. Or…any time really. Any time at all.

"Whatever." He sighed as he shook off the memories. What did it matter if she cut her hair — or if she shaved her head or dyed her eyelashes green, for that matter? He wasn't going to be around for more than a few days to see it anyhow. Nowadays, his home was almost three thousand miles away, and that suited him just fine. But, still, while he *was* here...

Was it selfish that he wanted her all to himself for awhile — no business, no awkwardness, no more inexplicable changes — just the two of them the way they'd always been? Too bad if it was, because that was exactly what he did want.

He couldn't have that now, but at least he could get away from Sassy and her disapproving glances. "C'mon in back," he said as he grabbed hold of Sophie's hand. "We can talk about what you want while I clean up — that way maybe everyone will be happy."

Declan guided Sophie back to the station he was using. She perched uneasily on the edge of the padded tattoo chair and watched while he cleaned up. The process was so ingrained he could have done it in his sleep. Slip the used needles into the sharps container, toss out the cups of leftover ink, strip the sleeves from his clip-cords, unwrap his machines, prep the tips, tubes and grips he'd used for the autoclave and spray every possible surface with disinfectant. Twice.

"So, how've you been?" he asked finally when it seemed the silence was going to last all evening.

Sophie's wistful smile disappeared. "Oh, you know..." She shrugged helplessly, a small frown creasing her brow. "Pretty good, I guess? Better every day?"

"Okay, well, that's good." She didn't sound too sure about that, however, and Declan found himself frowning as well. She didn't seem quite as happy to see him as he was to see her either. Out of all the unexpected changes he'd encountered since he'd been back in New Orleans, that hurt more than all of the others combined.

Had he done something to annoy her? It seemed unlikely. Unless he was misremembering, things between them hadn't ended badly. They hadn't actually ended at all. Not really. They'd both simply…moved on. He'd seen a chance to advance his career, and he'd taken it. At the time, he'd thought Sophie had been happy for him. He certainly hadn't planned on losing touch with her, but he'd been busy, preoccupied, and their friendship was just one of the many things he'd failed to keep up with. To be fair, she hadn't kept in touch with him, either.

"I really like your drawings," he said with a nod toward the sketches Sassy had given him. "That is your work, isn't it?"

Sophie's eyes lit up at that. She nodded. "I hoped you'd like them. I wasn't sure what I wanted at first. But once I knew *you* were going to be here, I just thought… Well, I guess it seemed like something that would fit in with…with what I've seen of your work."

"Yeah, it really does." Then the impact of what she'd said hit him. "You've been following my work?" Well, that was more like it.

"Oh, you know." Another blush hit Sophie's cheeks. She bit her lip. "Maybe. A little."

"Huh." Declan thought about that. He liked the idea that she'd been keeping up with what he was doing, but how, exactly, had she been doing that? Unless… "Whoa. Wait, wait, wait. You actually watch *my show*? Jeez, Sophie, I thought you had better taste than that. Hell, I don't even watch my show."

"I wouldn't say I *watch* it. But, you know, I've seen it a little. Maybe once or twice."

"You sure about that?" he teased. "You do know lying's still a sin, right? A bad girl like you oughta be more careful. I always figured your chances of getting into heaven were slim enough."

"And whose fault was *that*? As I recall, most of the sinning I did was the result of *you* talking me into things."

Sophie's chuckle was rough and throaty, just like it had always been, and Declan's body reacted to it the same way *it* always had. Like there was nothing in the world sexier than that laugh. Maybe there wasn't. Certainly he hadn't found anything that compared with it.

"I have no idea what you're talking about."

"Yeah, I'm sure. Anyway, don't go getting a swelled head. It's not like I make a habit of it. It's just, you know, if there's nothing better on and I'm flipping through channels...sure, I might stop and watch a few minutes."

"I call bullshit."Declan crossed his arms and leaned his hip against the counter. He couldn't keep from gloating. "'Fess up, Sophie. You watch the whole damn episode, don't you? Every. Single. Week."

"I only watch to see what you're gonna do next. I mean, holy shit, Declan, how do you get away with being such a jackass all the time? How is it no one's hauled off and punched you yet?"

"Oh, believe me, I've had more than a few close calls."

"Can't say I'm surprised to hear that."

"You do know it's mostly an act though, right? The audience expects it by now, so I have to keep it up. But I'm not *really* like that. At least not most of the time."

Sophie's expression softened. She met his worried gaze and smiled reassuringly. "I know."

"Good." Declan breathed out a sigh, feeling more relieved than he wanted to admit. "Meanwhile, however, I gotta say it again. I am *loving* the idea that you're such a big fan. You probably collect the merchandise and everything."

"Oh, please. In your dreams."

"Uh-huh and speaking of dreams, I bet you even sleep in one of the cast T-shirts. Is it one with my face on the front?"

"Pfft. As if." For the first time since she got there, Sophie looked relaxed. "Not that it's any of your business anymore, but my choice in sleepwear is the same as it's always been."

Which was to say she wore nothing at all. "I remember. One of my all-time favorite outfits." One he had every intention of seeing again soon. Tonight would be a good time. Maybe after dinner...or, hell, before dinner if he could manage it.

His mind made up, Declan straightened away from the counter. He grabbed the rolling stool he used for tattooing and pushed it over to the chair where she sat, positioning himself close enough so that he bracketed her legs with his own. "Okay, so, enough small talk. Tell me about this tattoo. What's the idea? I gotta say I'm a little surprised. I never would have figured you for the kind of woman who'd want an entire chest piece."

The smile disappeared from Sophie's face. "Yeah, well, me neither. But what can you do? Things change, right?" She shrugged and looked away from him. "I'm not sure what you want me to tell you. I don't know what the idea is either really. But that's not to say I haven't thought about doing something like this. I've been thinking about it for awhile, actually. It just wasn't urgent, you know? And, up until recently, I had enough to deal with. I sure didn't feel the need to take on anything more — especially not something that would require needles and weeks of healing. Been there, done that. You know?"

"Weeks," Declan scoffed. "What d'you mean weeks? This is *me* we're talking about. My tattoos are the shit—everyone knows that. They're legendary, the gold standard for healing. As long as you take care of it, it shouldn't take more than a week. Ten days max."

"Whatever." Sophie rolled her eyes. "I can see you're still as humble as ever. But, that wasn't really the point I was making. It was the flyer that convinced me. You know, the whole new beginnings thing? I figured maybe that was what I needed. I'm hoping this'll make me feel better about myself. Pretty, you know? So that when I look in the mirror I won't just see the scars or end up thinking about what I've lost. I'll see me, covered in flowers, wrapped up in a beautiful piece of art. And maybe that'll remind me to be grateful for what I still have. That I'm still here, I'm still alive; that life is good and...shit, I don't know. I hate it when I start sounding like a fucking greeting card. That's probably not even what you're asking about, is it?"

Declan didn't answer. His head felt as though it were on the verge of coming apart. His thoughts were in turmoil. He could barely hear himself think above the riotous rush of blood in his veins.

Sophie frowned. "Well? Am I wrong? C'mon, say something, damn it. Don't just sit there."

Scars? Still alive? Weeks of healing? Declan cleared his throat. "Sophie...what the fuck are you talking about? Why do you have scars?"

"Why do I have...?" Sophie's eyes grew wide. "Because of the cancer, Declan. Why do you think?"

"Cancer!"

"Breast cancer, yeah. In both breasts, 'cause, you know, I'm just so special that way. I had to have surgery. And...and chemo." She gestured at her head. "What the fuck are *you* talking about? I know you noticed!"

"I noticed your hair—yeah. You mean, that's why..."

"Exactly."

"Fuck."

She peered more closely at him. "How is this coming as a surprise to you? I mentioned it in the notes I sent along with the pictures. I assumed you got them. I even explained it on the phone. I thought... Jeez, didn't anyone tell you?"

"No." Declan shook his head, still unable to process the information. Maybe he should have known. Maybe he should have figured. Cancer survivors, amputees, that's mostly what they had on the scheduled for tomorrow, wasn't it? It was the night of the big fundraiser, after all.

And her hair—damn it, that should have been a dead giveaway. Dead. Holy shit. *She could have been dead.* His stomach heaved at the thought. No wonder it hadn't occurred to him. He probably hadn't wanted it to. Because, now that he knew...

He shoved the stool backward and got up quickly, unable to sit still any longer, not while every cell in his brain was demanding action, was insisting that he run. *Now. Go. Get out of here.*

"Declan?"

Go, goddamn it!

"Are you all right?" Sophie bit her lip and stared worriedly at him and that was probably the last straw. Declan couldn't handle the thought that *she* was worried about *him.* "I'm really sorry. I thought you knew."

"Just sit tight," he told her, although it was a miracle, at this point, that the words falling from his mouth made any sense at all. "I just gotta...I gotta... Fuck. I need a minute, okay? I'll be right back."

"Wait!"

It felt as though every eye in the room had been turned in his direction as he stumbled blindly from the room, knocking into things as he went. Voices followed him down the hall.

"Declan?"

"Hey! Where are you..."

"What the fuck, man?"

"Ross! Get your ass back here!"

He ignored them all. He could not do this here. *Would* not do this here. No way.

So what if he'd spent the last five years in a fishbowl? It had been his choice. He'd put his whole life on display, and he'd been fine with it. He'd exposed his flaws and his faults and his failings to the entire world, let them all watch from the comfort of their living rooms, week after week, as he fucked up and fell down again and again and again, but this? No way. Not happening. This was different. This was huge. And some things just fucking needed to stay private.

Chapter Four

Light spilled into the alley as the shop's back door was edged opened. Declan stayed right where he was, huddled on the curb at the base of the brick wall. Right next to the dumpster, next to the trash, where he felt like he belonged. He didn't even bother to look and see who had followed him outside. Whoever it was, he didn't want to talk to them.

Measured footsteps closed the small distance between them and stopped right in front of him. "Are you on a break or something?"

Sassy. Perfect. "Could you please just go away?"

"I brought you that coffee you said you wanted."

Declan tilted his head back to meet her gaze. "That's great. Thanks. Really. You're a fucking rock star. But I kinda want to be alone right now. So, if you don't mind, why don't you just turn around and take it back inside with you?"

"You do know you've still got a client waiting on you, right?"

"No shit." Sophie. Crap. Declan squeezed his eyes shut, his stomach still turning somersaults. *I could have lost her. She could have died.*

"I gotta say, I don't know exactly what's going on here with you two, but this behavior has to be some new kind of low, even for you."

"Even for me?" Declan felt his temper spike. "Wow. You *really* don't like me, do you?" He didn't care either way. Not really. Another week and he'd be back on the coast, and he'd never have to see her again anyway. But it did kind of surprise him when anyone didn't like him. Women especially.

Sassy didn't answer right away. It was dark and he couldn't really see her expression all that well, but based on her tone, he'd bet anything she was looking at him right now as though he was something she'd scraped off the bottom of her shoe. Which, come to think of it, would pretty much fit with how he was feeling.

He sighed again. "Okay, well... Whatever."

"Let me put it this way," Sassy said, finally breaking her silence. "I don't know you very well, so I can't say for sure, but on a scale of one to ten, where ten is my Mama and Jesus Christ, and one is Katrina, I'd rate you at about a six."

Katrina? Oh, hell no. She did not *just say that.* Declan clamped his mouth shut, choosing to ride out the inevitable wave of pain in silence. "Your scale's fucked up," he finally told her. "But you're right on one count. You don't know me at all."

"Which is why that six is provisional. For all I know, you could have a really good reason for being out here right now. Like maybe you got hit with a killer migraine or something. But it could also mean that you just don't give a shit about the fact that you're making that poor girl in there feel even worse *now* than you did when you were goin' on about her hair."

"Don't talk about her like that," Declan snapped. "You don't know the first thing about Sophie." Poor girl? Fuck that. Sophie would *hate* being pitied. One more reason he knew he'd made the right decision to come out here and hide. Pity, frustration, terror, disgust, he was caught in a storm of every ugly emotion he could name; and they kept piling up. Grief, denial, self loathing, despair, and a rage so deep he might never be over it. He didn't want Sophie reading any of that in his eyes and thinking it was for her. It wasn't.

He hated that this had happened to her — of course he did. But it was just one more example of how endlessly shitty life could be. The random unfairness of it all caught him by surprise, just like it always did, bringing a hurt that burned clear down to his soul.

He didn't pity Sophie. No, the only one he pitied in this scenario was himself. Because he hadn't known. Because she hadn't immediately turned to him when she'd gotten the bad news. Did it make him a selfish prick that his first thought was for himself? Maybe so. But it fucking killed him to think that he hadn't even rated a phone call.

How could she not have known that he'd want to be there for her? How could she not have realized what it would have done to him if he'd learned after the fact that he'd lost her?

"She should have told me she had cancer, damn it."

"Jesus, Declan, it's not about you!"

"Do you think I don't know that?" But maybe it should have been. At least a little. "We were friends, okay? We were more than friends. How come that didn't mean anything to her?"

"Maybe she didn't tell you because there was nothing you could have done. Maybe she didn't want to worry you."

"That's bullshit. Fuck that."

"Why? Why should she have told you? You weren't a couple, were you?"

Declan sighed. No. They hadn't been a couple. "It's complicated, all right? When we met…we weren't looking to settle down. I wasn't in a good place, and neither of us was ready to close the books on other relationships. So, no, we weren't a couple. We didn't make commitments or promises — hell, we didn't even keep in touch when I moved away." And what a mistake that had turned out to be. "But we were still friends, and she could have *died*! She could have *died*, damn it, and I wouldn't even have known."

"I'm sorry."

It had never even occurred to him that she wouldn't always be okay, that she wouldn't always be there. And, always, in the back of his head somewhere... "I guess I always thought that someday... Well, you know. "

"So why don't you go back inside and tell her that? Maybe she had a good reason for not contacting you. At the very least, you can still give her the nice tattoo she came here for."

"Ha." Declan laughed mirthlessly. "Yeah, I don't think so. That's not gonna happen. You're gonna have to find someone else for that."

"Is that a joke? I mean, it better be, because that's just not acceptable."

Declan met her gaze coolly. "It's not a joke. And you can glare at me all day long if you want to, but don't think for a minute that you're gonna change my mind. I can't, all right? There's a reason doctors don't operate on the people they care about. It's because they can't be trusted when their feelings are involved. This is exactly the same."

"Oh, it fucking is not the same. What the hell, Declan? That doesn't even make sense."

"Hey, you've got your scale of things that don't make sense, and I've got mine."

"You know, it's a good thing Henry Lee's not here right now. Because he'd for damn sure fire my ass for what I'm about to say. You artists need to check your egos at the door. No one's gonna *die* if you don't tattoo them, all right? I mean, on the scale of things that might actually be important in life, this doesn't even rate a number."

Declan shook his head. "You're wrong. It is important—especially to Sophie. Maybe you think I don't listen when people tell me about what they want. Maybe you think it's all about my own ego, about advancing my own career and the hell with everything else. And you know what? About half the time, you'd probably be right. But not this time. This isn't *nothing* to Sophie. This isn't like her other tattoos. Trust me, I was there when she got most of them, so I know what I'm talking about. She didn't come here today on a whim or because she was drunk or she lost a bet or her friends dared her to do it. This time she's looking for something that will make an actual difference to her life, something that'll change the way she feels about herself. She *needs* this. And I'm not the right person to do that for her."

"Of course you are! Who better to do it?"

"Why can't you understand this? It's not that I don't *want* to do it. It's not that I don't like the design or because it wouldn't be an awesome addition to my portfolio—because it definitely would. Under normal circumstances, I'd be knocking people down and climbing over bodies to get to be the one to do this tattoo. But I can't. I'm not saying no because I want to I'm saying no because I have to. I'm saying no because I. Can't. Do. It. I can't give her what she needs. And if you still don't get that...then I honestly don't know how to make it any more clear to you."

Sassy stood there for a moment, watching him, tapping her foot, still holding that stupid paper cup with the coffee he'd asked her for about a billion years ago. He supposed he should just be grateful she hadn't thrown it in his face yet. He could tell she was still thinking about it. But maybe, by the time she got around to actually doing it, the coffee would be too cold to do too much damage. "So are we done now?" he asked hopefully.

"Did you know she nearly changed her mind? About the tattoo, I mean. I was the one who first talked to her about it on the phone. We weren't thirty seconds into the conversation, and she was already trying to talk herself out of it—coming up with excuses, saying that maybe it wasn't such a good idea after all. I'd have bet a week's pay she wouldn't go through with it. But then I told her *you* were coming, and that made all the difference. I have to think she's here today at least partly because of the connection between you. I have to think that means more to her than you think it does."

"Maybe."

"No maybes about it."

Declan thought about that for a bit. "Okay, let's say you're right, just for the sake of argument. So what? How does that change anything?"

"Because if you back out now, she's not going to go through with it either."

"That's ridiculous. Sophie's not like that. She's not stupid—she'll understand. She'll want to have the best possible person tattooing her. Right now, that's not me."

"You know what, Declan? You can say that all you like. And you can sit there from now 'til Judgment Day pretending that it's all gonna turn out fine, that I can just suggest someone else and she's gonna be all 'yeah, that's great', but you'll only be fooling yourself. I've booked enough appointments to know when someone's having second thoughts about getting a tattoo. If you really believe this is important to her—and important *for* her, and if she's really as important to you as you claim she is, then I'm sorry, but I don't think you have a choice. You're gonna have to do it, Declan. You're just gonna have to suck it up and do it."

"And what if I can't do it, huh? You talk like it's so easy, but you have no idea what you're asking for. What if I mess up?" It was a stupid question, a fucking terrifying question. It hurt just hearing the words. The thought of disappointing Sophie, of maybe making things worse...it made him want to puke his guts out.

"Is that what this is about?" The confident tone in Sassy's voice made him furious. "Please. Why are you worrying about that? You won't mess up."

"You don't know that."

"Actually I do. Listen, you take tattooing as seriously as anyone I've ever met. And that's on the days when you don't actually give a fuck. There's no way you're going to mess this one up. Not when it means this much to you."

"Fuck." Declan felt as though he'd just heard his doom pronounced. He covered his face with his hands and cursed again. "Fuck!"

"Does that mean you know I'm right?"

Was she? He had no idea. "No, it means I want to punch something." In fact that wall behind him was beginning to look real attractive. Or maybe the dumpster. If he got lucky, maybe he would break one of his hands. It would be almost worth it. He'd like to see what Sassy would have to say then about his having no choice. But deep down he knew he wouldn't do anything to damage his hands. She was right about that at least. He *did* take his work seriously. And maybe it was just ego or maybe it was ambition or maybe it was some kind of fucked-up ideal—commitment to his art or some shit—but, yeah, she was right. He wouldn't fuck this up. He couldn't live with himself if he did. But that still didn't mean he could give Sophie what she needed.

"Okay, well, while you're exploring your Neanderthal impulses, let me tell you what *I'm* gonna do." She thought she'd won; Declan could hear it in her voice. "I'm gonna go bring your girl some coffee now and maybe buy you a little more time to pull yourself together. But if you're not back inside soon—and by soon I mean within the next five minutes—I'm gonna get Caliph to come out here and drag your sorry ass inside. Don't think I won't do it."

"Yeah, yeah. I hear you." Declan tipped his head back against the bricks, still trying to wrap his mind around this new reality. Somehow, he had to pull himself together. He had to clear his mind and go to work and give Sophie the tattoo she wanted. And it would be perfect. But would it be enough?

Chapter Five

The coffee Sophie had been drinking sat like a lead weight in her stomach. She glanced around, looking for someplace to dispose of her still half-full cup because there was no way she was ever going to finish it. Given the emphasis on cleanliness, how could there not be at least one trash can within easy reach? She wondered if anyone would notice if she just up and left?

She hadn't anticipated that it would be so hard for her to see Declan again—or for him to see her. She certainly hadn't imagined that he'd freak out the way he had. When it came to crises, he was pretty well jaded.

She was just gearing herself up to make a run for the front door when Declan came bustling back into the room, carrying a sheaf of stencils.

"Okay, here we go," he said, acting like nothing out of the ordinary had happened.

She stared at him in surprise as he spread the papers out on the counter. She recognized them at once as copies of her own drawings.

"I thought I was going to have to re-draw some of these to make them fit," he told her. "But now I don't think that will be necessary. I think they're actually going to work out fine just the way they are. We may have to re-size a few, but that won't be a problem, and besides that's mostly up to you. You might not want to do that either. I made them all as separate stencils so we could play around with them a little. All we really have to decide on is the placement of them."

Sophie let herself relax a little. "Wow. You've done your homework, huh?"

"Of course I did," Declan replied absently, his attention on the stencils as he moved them around on the countertop, as though searching for an arrangement that pleased him. "You heard what I told Sassy. I've been excited about this tattoo from the start."

Yes. He had said that. But that was before she'd dropped her bombshell. Sophie couldn't help but notice that he'd been avoiding her gaze ever since he'd come back into the room. So he couldn't even look at her now? What was up with that?

Maybe she was overreacting. Maybe he was just preoccupied. But suddenly there was too much tension between them and she needed to get away from it. She stood and picked up her purse. "Okay, well, placement, that's the easy part, right? I mean we don't really even have to decide on that today, do we?"

"Not really, no. I mean, we could, but it's not really critical. They're just a guide anyway. As long as we're on the same page and you're happy with the sizes and all... I'll probably end up free-handing some of the elements anyway."

"Good. Fantastic. Sounds like a plan." It had been a shock for him; she got that. He probably needed some time to adjust. If she left now, he'd have almost twenty-four hours before he had to tattoo her. Hopefully, that would be time enough for him to get over...whatever this was. "Then I guess we're done for now."

"Yeah." Finally, Declan's eyes met hers. "So...whaddaya think? You wanna go grab some dinner with me?"

"Dinner?"

"Or drinks, I guess, if you're really not hungry. I kinda hope you are though, because I'm starving."

"I don't know..."

"Oh, come on, Sophie Jane. Why not, huh? I've really missed you. I want to hear more about what's been happening with you. I have the feeling there's a lot we need to catch up on."

"A heart to heart?" Sophie couldn't help grimacing. "Now? Oh, please, let's not." She did not want to discuss anything while he was in this kind of mood—especially not that. She did not want him feeling sorry for her or making her feel any more sorry for herself. She needed the old Declan tonight, the one who usually thought only about himself and who she could always count on to distance himself emotionally whenever things got even a little bit rough.

"Just dinner then, all right? Please? You know you want to..." And there it was. The tiny half smile, the sexy pitch to his voice, that look in his eyes that promised it would be well worth her while to give him whatever he wanted. She never had been able to resist that look.

Sophie sighed in surrender. "Sure. Why not? Dinner sounds good." But she knew it wouldn't end with dinner. It never did...

Just as she'd expected, dinner led to drinks, which led to a nostalgic visit to that little jazz place over on Frenchmen Street where they always used to go, which led to even more drinks. From there it was just a short walk back to the hotel where Declan was staying, in an extravagant, two-story suite with shuttered French doors and a balcony that looked down on Bourbon Street. It was the kind of place he could never have afforded five years ago. The kind of place neither of them would ever have thought to stay in.

"This place is amazing," she'd said as she turned away from that view, just in time to catch an even better one—that of Declan pulling his shirt off over his head. Her mouth went dry. *Omigod. Talk about amazing.* The past five years had clearly been kind to more than just Declan's bank account. She didn't think she'd ever seen him so healthy and fit. It could be he spent all his off time working out in the gym, she supposed, although the sun-bronzed tone of his skin suggested otherwise.

As he turned to toss his shirt onto a nearby chair, the tattoo emblazoned on his left shoulder blade caught her eye. The large Celtic cross, with '*Ross*' inscribed above it and three sets of dates beneath, brought her back down to earth with a bone-jarring thump. There were still some things that hadn't changed, that never could change. The boy came with baggage. Heaps of it.

In fact, the only major difference between now and years ago was that, this time around, they *both* had scars. She wondered if the ones you couldn't see were still the hardest to deal with.

That alone probably should have had her running for the door. But somewhere along the way Sophie had decided to stop worrying about any of it—at least for tonight. She didn't care where they were headed, where they'd end up, or how things could possibly work out between them now when they'd never worked before. She'd worry about that tomorrow.

She already knew where they'd end up tonight. If she was lucky, they'd end up in his bed. And, if there was any justice at all in the universe, she also knew how things would work out—in exactly the same way they'd always done, with her feeling very, very satisfied. She'd have to be crazy not to jump on that. Crazy, or a lot more sober than she was feeling at the moment...

Now, just a short while later, she was halfway to her goal, propped up on her elbows on the bed, naked from the waist down, while an already completely naked Declan lay stretched between her spread thighs. He stared at her pussy with the kind of rapt attention that made her want to beg him to *stop looking already and touch me, please, please touch me — yes, there, now.*

"God, Sophie, look at you. Look how wet you are." He reached out and ran a single finger up the length of her cleft. "Jeez, you're dripping for me. I fucking love that."

Something about the awestruck tone of his voice made her giggle, although that could have been the absinthe too, come to think of it. "Well, you know, it has been kind of awhile since I've done this with anyone, so..." It really wasn't all that surprising. Actually, it was more than a little depressing. *Stop thinking. Don't wanna think about that right now.*

"Sophie Jane." Declan glanced up with a scandalized expression. "What is *wrong* with you? You never want to tell a man something like that. You should *always* make me think it's because of me, that you're wet for *me*, that *I'm* the reason you're about to soak through this duvet."

"Aw, poor Declan." More giggles threatened to erupt. "Will the hotel charge you extra for that?" She fought down the laughter and put on her most serious face. "You know I'm *always* wet for *you*."

"Uh-huh. That's better." Declan lowered his head to press a soft kiss against her inner thigh. "That's what I want to hear."

"But...it has been a really, *really* long time."

Declan's eyes danced with mirth. "Brat. Now you're gonna be sorry. You do know you're going to pay for that, don't you?"

"Oh, God, I hope so." Sophie fell back upon the pillows, giggling once again. Oh, how she'd missed this. She'd missed it so much: the teasing, the playfulness, the control — just Declan being Declan. Even if it couldn't last, even if he was only doing this to prove some kind of point or as an act of misplaced nostalgia, why should she care? It was still one perfect moment in time, and who knew if she'd ever feel this way again? Why shouldn't she allow herself to enjoy it? It was only a few days after Christmas, after all. Why couldn't she look at this night with Declan in the same way she'd been looking at her tattoo: as a flashy and extravagant, only-slightly-belated Christmas present to herself. Ho ho ho.

When her giggles threatened to give way to tears, she took a couple of deep breaths in an attempt to center herself. A heavy silence from the bottom of the bed drew her attention. She raised her head to find Declan staring at her face with an expression she couldn't fathom.

She frowned. "What? Why are you looking at me that way?"

He didn't answer, just surged up to cover her body with his. Instinctively, she moved her arms inward, shielding her chest. The hair that dusted his pecs bristled against her palms as he kissed her with exquisite gentleness. All this tenderness was more than a little unnerving.

Sophie pushed at his chest in an effort to dislodge him. "What are you doing? Stop that. I'm not dying, you know."

"What?" Declan lifted his head and stared at her with an alarmed expression.

"I am not dying," she repeated, adding when he didn't respond right away. "You seemed worried."

"I seemed... Jesus, Sophie. Why wouldn't I worry about you? Why would you even say something like that?"

"Because it's true. And because I want you to stop it. You don't *have* to worry. Really. My last blood tests were all normal. I think my doctors were very encouraged by that."

"Sophie," Declan growled. He sat up and looked at her sternly. "You need to stop talking right now."

Sophie was happy to oblige. She shut her mouth and gazed up at him. Expectant. Hopeful. Only the littlest bit dizzy. Until he took hold of her wrists and attempted to lift her arms over her head and the whole room began to spin. Her stomach quivered suddenly, but not in that pleasant way she'd come to expect.

All the drinks she'd consumed this evening and that, so far, had been contributing to her pleasantly intoxicated mood seemed to slosh violently around inside her. Sophie shuddered, trying to pull away, trying to break his hold on her. The weakness in her muscles made that almost impossible, and the resultant feeling of helplessness had her once again on the verge of tears. "Let me go."

Declan released her immediately. He sat back on his heels and gazed at her quietly for a moment, his eyes dark and troubled. "Take your shirt off." It was too gentle to be an order, but what did that matter? Order, suggestion, demand, request—however he meant it, there was no way she could give him that tonight.

"Nuh-uh." She shook her head, feeling suddenly no more than twelve years old, wishing he wasn't *right there*, looming over her, his big body wedged between her legs. She wrapped her arms around her middle, more aware than usual of the slight tremors that so often affected them, particularly when she was feeling stressed or anxious or if she pushed too hard.

She wished she didn't feel quite so vulnerable. Even with her shirt on, she felt more naked and exposed than she ever had before with him. And again: not in a good way. What the fuck was she even doing here?

"Why not, huh?" Declan's voice sounded even more gentle than before. "You know you're going to have to let me see you sometime, right? And I am tattooing you tomorrow..."

"Yeah, but that's *tomorrow*," Sophie replied. "Right now, I just want to pretend none of it ever happened, that it's just you and me — same as always. And that everything is still exactly like it used to be."

One corner of his mouth curved upward in the smallest of smiles. "Used to be I'd have had you naked by now."

"Please. I'm asking, all right? This isn't a joke."

"I know." His lips tightened as thought he'd thought better of what he'd been about to say, as though he were trying to keep the words in, but then they came blurting out all the same. "I hate that I wasn't there for you, that I didn't even know what was happening. How come you didn't call me? I would have dropped whatever I was doing to be there for you. You had to have known that."

Sophie sighed loudly. "God, Declan, would you stop already? You would not. You know you wouldn't have. Things were going too well for you. You were having too good a time out there with your show. And, besides, there was *nothing* you could have done. I hate that you're making me sound so pathetic. Yeah, the diagnosis threw me. The surgery, the recovery, the chemo — all of it sucked. I swear I never want to be in a hospital again. But it's not like I had to go through it all on my own. I had plenty of support. My family was with me for most of it, so, you know — Oh, shit." She stopped suddenly. Declan's face had gone blank, wiped clear of emotion. It was a closed-in expression she knew all too well. A wave of shame swept over her. "Oh, my God. Oh, Declan..." She was sure her own face must've turned bright red. Suddenly, she wasn't feeling nearly as drunk as she would have liked. "Sweetie, I'm so sorry."

"It's all right. Forget it." He let out a deep breath and then leaned in close — close enough to touch his forehead to hers. His weight rested on his forearms. His big hands gently cradled her head. "That's not..." His voice faltered and he had to take a deep breath before continuing. "That's not what's important right now, all right? Let's just — "

"Of course it's important!" Sophie slid one hand up, just far enough so that her finger tips could make contact with his cheek. "I just wasn't thinking! You know I'd never hurt you like that. Not on purpose."

She felt his jaw clench. "Not now, Soph. Don't wanna talk about it. Don't want to talk about *anything* right now." Then he made sure of her compliance by sealing her mouth in a long, hard, heated kiss.

There'd never been anyone who'd kissed her like Declan did, with all the passionate intensity he put into his art. It was as though he put his whole being, everything he had, into his kiss. Not every kiss, of course. Not even most of them, sadly. He kept everyone at a distance far too much of the time. But every once in awhile, he let loose and kissed her like he was doing now, with his tongue sliding along hers, stealing her breath, stealing her mind, acting like he could never get enough of her. She could never get enough of him, either — which had always been her problem.

Frustrated whimpers purled up her throat. She wanted so much more from him. She always had — more than he could give her. Right now, she wanted her arms wrapped around his neck, her fingers tangled in his hair. She wanted to stretch and arch beneath him and give herself over to him completely. But she couldn't. Her arms refused to budge. Her back refused to arch. Her body wanted to curl in on itself and disappear. All these months later, and her first instinct was still to hide. Who knew if that would ever change?

"I would have dropped whatever I was doing to be there for you."

"You would not. You were having too good a time."

The words they'd just spoken kept repeating in Declan's mind. He supposed he shouldn't be too surprised. Why would Sophie not think something like that? Hadn't he been off having a good time when his brother was killed, when his grandfather died? But he'd already beaten himself up for that more times than he could count. That horse was as dead as it was ever going to get.

Still, it hurt that she hadn't known better, that she hadn't trusted him more. And her ongoing distrust? That really hurt. Had it really not occurred to her that they both might have changed in the past five years? Or did she just not care?

Determined to make her care, to get some reaction out of her, some sense she still remembered how good they'd been together, he broke their kiss and slid back down her body to nestle, once more, between her thighs. He would have loved to stop and explore along the way, find out exactly what she was hiding beneath those annoying layers of fabric, but that would happen soon enough. And maybe she was right. Maybe one night of remembering how things used to be, of mourning the past and finding closure, was what they both needed. He'd been running from his past. Did she understand he hadn't meant to run from her?

Or was he still lying to himself?

He pushed those thoughts away and focused instead on a part of her that hadn't changed. Or hadn't changed much. Five years ago, her mound had been totally bare. Now, as he'd already discovered when he was down here a moment earlier, she'd allowed a small patch of curls to grow in — reddish-gold, a little darker than the hair on her head. He buried his nose in her thatch and breathed deep, inhaling her own unique fragrance. Essence of Sophie. That hadn't changed at all. Spicy and clean — it was still the most mouth-watering scent he'd ever encountered. He thumbed her lips apart, holding her open for his tongue.

He loved the way she bucked and cursed and begged for more when he used the flat of his tongue on her clit. Loved the way her legs trembled, how they tightened around his shoulders giving him a heartfelt hug that totally made up for that botched affair in the shop. Clearly this was how they should have been greeting each other all along.

"Close," Sophie rasped out as he pulled away. "So close. Oh, fuck, Declan, don't stop now."

"Wouldn't dream of it." Her words spurred him on. He used his fingers to spread her pussy open then wriggled closer, forcing her legs wide as well. "Gonna make you come *bébé*," he murmured just before his lips latched onto her clit. He teased and tongued the little nub, then took it in his mouth and sucked. Sophie rocked her hips, thrusting herself against him. In another moment, she'd be coming in his mouth.

He pulled off to look at her—all flushed and juicy and ready. Ready for him. He slipped two fingers inside those pouty little lips and pumped several times. He loved watching as his fingers disappeared into her flesh and re-emerged slick and shiny. He loved the soft, sucking sounds her body made, the way her swollen lips pulled at his flesh, clinging, wanting.

"Please," she begged, drawing the single word out.

Leaning in once more, he sucked that luscious, hot pearl back into his mouth. Her cunt tightened around his fingers, tighter, tighter, tighter, so that with every plunge, the fit became a little more snug.

Then, with no other warning than that, she came. Her body convulsed. Her hands clasped his head, holding him in place. Declan rode out the tremors, licking softly at her clit until she pushed him away.

He lifted his head and looked at her. Her face was flushed. Her chest rose and fell with each breath. "Fuck me," she gasped. "Come up here and fuck me now."

But Declan had other ideas. He slid his hands beneath her and lifted her hips, giving him access to the sweet pucker of her asshole. To that part of her body that, more than anything else, he considered his.

He'd been the one who'd introduced her to the joys of anal play, the one who taught her how to take first a plug then his fingers and finally his cock. He'd been the first to fuck her ass, to feel the way those tight muscles seized his cock in a heart-stopping grip when she came. The first, yes, but not the last. And, for that, he had no one but himself to blame.

He'd meant what he told Sassy; they were never a couple, never exclusive. He didn't do forever. Forever was nothing but a lie. He and Sophie were friends with benefits, fuck buddies. He hadn't wanted anything else.

What he *had* wanted, however, more often than not toward the end, was to call her up, late at night, after he was sure both their dates had gone home. He'd make her tell him all the details of her evening—where she'd gone and who she'd done. And, no matter how many times he'd already come that night, he'd lie in bed and jack himself off while her voice in his ear gave him every dirty detail.

Jealousy had no place in their relationship. That's what he told himself, what he'd told them both. He never would have admitted how pathetic he'd become, how often he pretended it was all just make-believe. That she was only telling him what he wanted to hear. That, in reality, she'd spent the night at home, all alone, waiting for his call, making up the stories she'd tell him.

It occurred to him now that, perhaps, that had played a part in why he'd never called her in the past five years. Perhaps he knew that, at a distance of two thousand miles, her voice would only make him homesick. Perhaps he feared that the stories she'd tell him would feel too real, or that she wouldn't tell him anything, having found another playmate, someone whose secrets she'd keep to herself, not share with him…

Declan ran his tongue along the crease of Sophie's ass. "Wanna take you here," he told her.

"Omigod." She sighed. "Oh, Declan…" Her tone was so breathlessly enthusiastic he couldn't help but smile.

"Can I?" he asked, already sure of her answer even as he paused to tease the small opening. "Can I flip you over and put you on your knees and fuck your ass until you scream for me?"

"God, yes. Hurry." Her response was immediate, unequivocal, exactly what he'd expected. And then she sighed. "No. Wait. Probably not."

"What?" Declan glanced up at her. It wasn't just the words that surprised him; he was startled by the way the sexual tension seemed to have drained right out of her body. "Probably *not*?"

Sophie blushed. "My arms aren't as strong as they used to be. Anything where I have to hold myself up for any length of time is probably out for the time being. Sorry."

"Yeah. Me too." His answer was automatic. He cringed when he heard the words coming out of his mouth. "Shit. I mean, no. Don't be. It's no big deal. We can do whatever you want." He hated that this had happened to her. Hated that there seemed to be no end to the changes, the restrictions, the loss she had to deal with. Hated that he hadn't been there for her—so that now he didn't know enough to keep from shooting himself in the foot every time he opened his mouth.

"Whatever I want, huh?" Sophie regarded him thoughtfully. "All right then. Get up."

Declan scrambled to his feet, painfully aware of his hard-on, heavy and full and pointing right at her. Sophie sat up. She grabbed a pillow and slid to the edge of the bed. She dropped the pillow to the floor, and then dropped to her knees on top of it.

Her eyes gleamed darkly when she looked up at him and smiled. "This is what I want. Her hand closed around his shaft. "Your cock in my mouth. It's been a long time."

It had been a very long time. And Declan was all too happy to help rectify that. Still…"Are you sure you're all right down there?"

Sophie nodded, but her gaze was on his cock and on her hand sliding up and down along the length of it. "Yes, but I might need you to do some of the work," she said as she swiped her thumb over the head of his cock, spreading wetness. "You might have to feed it to me. I might need you to fuck my mouth."

Declan groaned. "Oh, I'll feed it to you all right." He'd forgotten how hot it always made him when she talked like that. How had he forgotten that?

He cupped the back of her head with one hand and wrapped the other around his cock. "Suck me a little first. Get me nice and wet."

Sophie grinned. She grasped hold of his hips with both hands and allowed him to direct her closer. Her lips closed over him. She sucked the crown of his cock into her mouth.

As her tongue flickered along the crest, Declan found himself frowning. "What happened to your tongue piercing?" Damn it, he hated all these changes. Five years…it had felt like no time at all while he was gone. Now that he was back, it seemed like several lifetimes had passed.

Sophie pulled back, shrugging out from under his hand. She glanced up at him crossly. "I had to take it out for the surgery. They're fussy about those things. I could have put it back in later, but the hole had closed up by the time I thought about it and..." Another shrug. "Oh, you know."

Declan's erection flagged. No. He didn't know. "So, what are you saying? You didn't want to re-pierce it? Or you couldn't for some reason?" It wasn't just idle curiosity. He had a reason for asking. Piercing took a toll on a weak immune system. So did tattoos — especially large tattoos. If she still wasn't strong enough for the one, she wasn't getting the other. Not from him, not from anyone, not if he had anything to say about it. That was non-negotiable.

"I could've. Like I said, I thought about doing it. But then I thought about everything that was involved — the clamps, the antiseptic, the recovery time." She shuddered. "It just seemed like too much bother."

"But it wasn't because of health issues? You're certain?"

Sophie scowled. "I told you before: I'm fine. It was... Oh, call it a déjà vu issue if you want. I'd been there; I'd done that. I decided enough was enough."

Declan nodded. "Okay. Fair enough. I just needed to know that you're really okay," he said as he reached for her once more. "You're important to me."

Sophie's expression softened. "You're important to me too. And I'm really okay." Then she proceeded to prove it by taking him all the way to the back of her throat.

The sight of her pretty lips wrapped around his cock, the bite of pain from her nails when they dug into his butt, the hot slide of her tongue along his shaft as she took him deep — it all combined to have Declan coming far more quickly than he wanted.

Afterward, they cuddled together in bed, but it wasn't long before Sophie was slipping out from beneath Declan's arm.

He snuggled into the pillows, feeling more peaceful and content than he had in a very long time. The only thing missing was Sophie. He could hear her moving around the room and he wanted to tell her to stop whatever it was she was doing and come back to bed, but he was too blissfully exhausted to move or even speak. They needed to talk; he knew that too. Christ, they needed to talk about all sorts of things, his feelings, his regrets, her cancer...

Experience told him those were the kinds of thing it would be a mistake to ignore for too long. Unfortunately, they were also the very things he did not even want to think about right now.

Sophie leaned over him from behind and he sighed in pleasure as he was surrounded once again by her warmth and her sweet perfume. Yes. This was better. This was definitely more like it. As she braced her small hand on his shoulder and kissed his cheek, the front of her blouse brushed against his back, and he was all at once acutely aware of what he couldn't feel: the soft press of her breasts. His heart ached with loss. His hands still remembered the feel of her. His tongue still remembered her taste. It killed him to think he'd never know those pleasures again. He could only imagine how she felt about it.

He took hold of her hand. He had no right to ask, but he did anyway. "Stay. Don't go."

"Can't," she said. "Gotta get back to Lagniappe."

Declan frowned. "What? You're getting me a lagniappe? Can't it wait 'til morning?"

"No." Sophie laughed. She smacked him lightly on his shoulder. "Lagniappe's my roommate's cat. Anyway, you've already had enough 'little extras' for one night."

Declan reached for her again, but she shrugged him off. "Don't get greedy," she told him. Smiling, she pulled away from him. She made it look easy. And maybe for her it was. "I'll see you tomorrow."

Chapter Six

New Year's Eve...

Sophie glanced around the tattoo shop. It looked almost exactly the same as it had yesterday—which was no huge surprise. The only change was the addition of a couple of *shoji* screens that had been set up around the station where Declan would be tattooing her. She hadn't really thought about it, but she was glad he had. She could do without people standing around staring at her. She'd have been even happier if she could have figured out a way to get this done without Declan seeing her either. Clearly, some of the things she wanted in life were impossible. Okay, most things really.

There was also a mirror on a stand, angled toward the padded table—another change she wasn't sure what to think of. She supposed the idea was so that she could see herself while Declan was working on her. That was probably the last thing she wanted to do.

"Why don't you hop up on the table now and take off your shirt," Declan suggested.

Sophie shuddered as she was hit with an odd feeling, almost déjà vu. The request itself, the matter-of-fact tone of his voice, it all sounded a little too much like the doctor's appointment where her cancer had first been discovered. Her stomach roiled, although whether that was caused by the first waves of an incoming panic attack or last night's drinks still rocketing around in her system, she couldn't tell. She felt a little like she'd gotten caught in some bizarre kind of time loop where the same things would just keep happening over again, and each time she'd lose a little more of herself.

"Sophie?"

"Yeah, okay," she replied, still hesitating. She couldn't make herself get up on that table.

"There's nothing to be nervous about." Declan's voice sounded even more calm now — she hadn't thought that was even possible.

"Oh, sure. Says the person who's going to be poking me with needles in a few minutes. Nothing *at all* to be nervous about there."

Declan's eyes twinkled at that. "As I recall, you always enjoyed a little pain play."

"Not helping," Sophie replied sternly. Although, really, it was. That was true. And the fact that Declan would be the one dishing it out was even better. She took a deep breath and unbuckled the belt she had fastened over her shirt. She glanced around again. "Where should I put this?"

Declan held out a hand. "Give it here." He took it in both hands and snapped it a couple of times, smiling wickedly as he did. The sharp crack of the leather caused an odd sort of quietness to settle in Sophie's gut. Her skin flushed — her mind going exactly where he wanted it to — and she had to look away. She pulled the shirt over her head and handed that to him as well.

Now she was down to just a camisole. Static electricity had messed up her hair, so she took a moment to smooth her hands over her head, patting everything back in place, not thinking about the next step. And trying *very* hard not to think of the fact that, even though he hadn't seen the worst of it yet, there was no more disguising the fact that her breasts were gone. He couldn't possibly have missed that fact, not now that she was dressed in only a single layer of thin silk. She hated the thought of him seeing her like this.

She wrapped her arms around herself as though she could hide from him. She hated that the simple act or crossing her arms was so easy now. Her arms should *not* be able to reach so far around her waist. Her breasts should be there, getting in the way, plumped up by her arms, swelling over the top of her cami, drawing his attention.

When her gaze met Declan's once again, he shook his head and said, even more gently, "Honey, you're gonna have to lose the tank as well."

"I'm getting there." Sophie fought down another wave of nausea. She had to turn her back to him before she could strip the shirt off over her head. In that first moment when he saw her, it was important that her eyes not be obscured. If she could, she wouldn't do this at all. But since she *was* doing it, she was damn well going to witness his reaction. She knew he'd flinch. She really hoped he wouldn't, but she *knew* he would. And if he did, *when* he did... She didn't really know if she could go through with this.

She took another deep breath and turned back around to face him, holding her top against her chest. When she dropped it, he showed almost no reaction. His eyes narrowed briefly, then he gazed dispassionately at her body for a long, long moment, tilting his head from side to side, gaze flicking from her to the stencils in his hand and back again. Finally, he nodded and said, "Yeah. Yeah, okay. I think that will work. Let's do this."

Talk about anticlimactic! Sophie felt her temper spike. "That's it? That's all you have to say about it?"

Declan shrugged. "What do you want me to say? It's not as bad as I was expecting?"

Oh, was that so? "Well, maybe you should try viewing it from this angle."

"But if I did that, how would I tattoo you?"

"Funny." She knew she was being unreasonable. She hadn't wanted him to flinch, and he hadn't. But she still wasn't happy with his reaction. She would have probably felt better if he'd called her on her bratty attitude, but they were talking about her *breasts*. She missed them. She wanted them back. As for Declan... Well, she'd kind of thought that *he* might've missed them too, at least a little bit.

Or maybe not. In all likelihood, one set was pretty much the same as another to him.

"C'mon, *bébé*. I've got a busy night ahead of me, so let's get started. This is going to be beautiful. Hop up on the table and let me get these stencils in place."

Sophie eyed the table with a worried glance. "I might need a little help with that," she finally admitted reluctantly. "It's kind of high."

Declan seemed to freeze for an instant. A stricken expression flashed across his face, and then he sighed and shook his head. "Girl, I see right through you. You really have to stop making up such flimsy excuses."

"What excuses?" Sophie glared at him as he took a step closer. "I told you last night, I don't have the upper body strength I used to."

Declan's hands settled around her waist, fingers lightly caressing her skin. "I call bullshit. I'm thinking you'll just use any old excuse to get my hands on you again."

Sophie gaped at him as he lifted her onto the table. Her heart hammered as he leaned in close to whisper, "And that's exactly what you'll be getting in another couple of minutes. My hands. All over you. Just like they were last night." Then he tilted her chin up and kissed her, soft and sweet. There was a twinkle in his eyes as he straightened away from her. He tapped the tip of her nose with his finger and smiled. "So relax, okay? 'Cause you know you're in good hands."

When he'd turned away to get the stencils, Sophie cleared her throat. "So. Do you always sexually harass your customers?"

Declan shook his head. "Not always, no. Mostly it's just the ones I like." He turned back again, papers in hand. "Okay, you ready?"

"As I'll ever be." She took a couple of deep, calming breaths as Declan smoothed the stencils into place. Positioning each one just so. When he lifted them away, faint traces of purple ink remained. He repositioned the mirror so she could see them.

"That look all right?" he asked.

The déjà vu was back. Visions of skin being marked for surgery flooded Sophie's mind. She glanced away quickly. "It's great. Let's do it."

Declan cupped her cheek. "It's just a guide. The actual tattoo won't look like this, you know. It's going to be beautiful. I promise."

Sophie allowed herself a moment to just luxuriate in his touch. "I know." That was the one thing she wasn't worried about. Declan never did anything halfway.

The vinyl of the table was cold against Sophie's skin as she lay on her back and tried to get comfortable. Declan tested out his equipment. The buzz of his machine was reassuringly familiar, reminding her that this was not the first tattoo he'd given her. But the first line burned like fire, which was not at all what she'd expected. Sophie gasped in surprise. She hadn't remembered it feeling like this.

Declan grimaced apologetically. "These thin little needles can really sting. But don't worry. This is only for the fine details—the ones you did in pen and ink."

Sophie groaned. "Oh, good. I'm glad there weren't a lot of those."

"Exactly."

If she'd had any idea what it would lead to, she'd have left all the details off altogether.

"Just try and relax, all right? It will hurt less."

"Easy for you to say."

"Yes it is," Declan replied somewhat absently, his eyes focused once more on his work. "But it's also true."

Sophie tried her best to follow his suggestions, but it all went to hell when Declan's needle skated over her ribcage, drawing a grunt of pain from her lips. Relaxing was impossible. She sucked in a quick breath and just barely refrained from cursing out loud — not that anyone would have heard her above the music pounding out over the shop's speakers, no doubt exactly the reason they played it so loud.

"I know. Sorry. Ribs are a bitch."

"So I've heard." It seemed like the kind of thing he said at least once in almost every episode. "Honestly, I think I've lost track of how many times you've said that."

Declan nodded absently. "Yeah, no kidding. Me too." Then he paused. A silly smile broke over his face. He glanced up at her. "Aha! You do watch. I knew it."

"Shut up, you jerk. Stop gloating." She wasn't so sure it was her ribs that were the problem, and, if she were honest, she doubted it would be over soon. After all this time, she hadn't expected that it would still freak her out this much to have someone touch her there, even now, so long after her surgery.

She was just so thankful it was Declan. How could she ever have imagined she could handle this with anyone else?

"Everything all right?" he asked as he paused to wipe down the area he'd been working on.

Sophie nodded. "I'm just glad it's you."

Declan glanced up at her questioningly. "What's that?"

"Doing this. I don't think I could have gone through with it otherwise."

Declan's gaze softened. "I'm glad too." Then he switched machines and dipped his needle into a small cup of red ink. "Now comes the fun part," he said with a smile.

Within minutes, bright splashes of color had begun to make their appearance. Sophie caught glimpses in the mirror, amazed at how closely it paralleled her initial vision. There was only one problem with "the fun part". It took time.

"How are you doing?" Declan asked an eternity later, eyes focused on his work. "You still okay?"

"I could use a little distraction," Sophie admitted. She wasn't sure she'd ever seen him so quiet before. She was beginning to regret having told him to shut up. Had he finally learned to follow directions? Who knew!

"There was something I wanted to tell you last night," Declan began, after another long pause. "You left before I had the chance. I wanted to say that I would have come back, if you'd asked me to. I know you think I wouldn't, but I would've."

Sophie cringed as she recalled their conversation last night and some of the things she'd said. But who was he kidding? "Good to know. I promise I'll keep that in mind next time it comes up."

Declan shut off his machine and stared at her. "Next time?"

"Kidding."

"So there's no chance... You aren't expecting a...a reoccurrence, are you?"

"Well, not in my breasts, that's for sure. I think I'm pretty much in the clear on that front."

"Sophie." Declan's voice was grim. He didn't even react to her pun. That really pissed her off.

She glared at him. How dare he act so serious when she was struggling to keep things light? "How do you want me to answer that, Dec? How does anyone know what the future holds? Life is just one surprise after another sometimes. Hell, *you* know that!"

Declan nodded. Yeah. He knew all right. "Story of my life," he said, because it sort of was…

After his father's death, Declan and his brother had gone to live with their grandfather. Mama had been having a hard enough time dealing with them even before her husband offed himself. Declan didn't blame her too much for that. He and Dev had been a handful—that was no lie. She'd eventually moved to Texas and gotten remarried. Pretty much the only thing she'd left her sons was the title to their father's Camaro.

They'd had big plans for that car back in the summer of '05. The twentieth Burning Man Festival was taking place at the tail end of August; they were going to drive out there and be a part of history.

Until Pappaw fell and broke his hip just a few weeks before they were set to leave. Obviously, someone would have to stay and take care of him. Declan and his brother settled the question of who in the same way the Ross men had always settled important matters. Over a game of darts.

Declan had won. A lucky throw. He'd taken their car and headed west. And at just about the same time that he'd come rolling into Black Rock City, Hurricane Katrina had rolled over New Orleans.

He'd never really learned all the details of what had happened; he never would. He could guess a lot of it though. Pappaw was a stubborn old man. He wouldn't have been keen on evacuating his home—even if he could have walked. If Declan had been there, he and Dev probably could have succeeded in manhandling their grandfather into the Camaro's front seat, but it wouldn't have been easy. On his own and without a vehicle? Devlin wouldn't have stood a chance.

The old man's body was found floating in the street. Devlin survived long enough to end up in the Superdome, where he'd taken a knife to the ribs in the course of some stupid-ass brawl and bled out in the mud.

By all accounts, his brother had gone a little crazy, even before the fight. Declan never doubted it. He'd gone pretty crazy himself in the months that followed.

He was the last of the Ross men. He was the last of the Rosses altogether, unless you counted his mama, which he didn't. He had lost his tribe, his family, and a large part of his own identity. With so little left, he was no longer sure who he was — only who he wasn't. He wasn't a twin anymore, and he'd never been anything else.

It was a tattoo that saved his sanity — or at least some part of it. Somehow, having an ever-present reminder of his loss, right there on his shoulder, where he could reach back and touch it, gave shape to his grief. It kept the pain in his heart from completely taking over his mind.

He'd found solace in designing his tattoo with its intricate Celtic interwoven style; he'd thought about those he'd lost the whole time he was drawing it. His father, his grandfather, his brother, his memories of them bled into every line. The initial pain as their memorial was etched into his skin, the ache that lingered for days afterward while his torn skin knitted itself back together, gave him closure. As the tattoo healed, so had his heart.

He was left with an unshakable belief in the power of tattoos to transform and heal. When Shep commented favorably on the quality of his artwork, it was as though a beam of light had shined down from the heavens. Declan knew he had found his path in life. Tattooing had provided him with an outlet for his creativity, a focus for his attention. It gave him a way to bring beauty to the world's ugliness. The fact that it had also given him a damn good income was not completely inconsequential either.

It wasn't the money that he was thinking about right now, however. He was thinking about the comfort and healing he could give Sophie—and the others he'd be tattooing tonight. Along with closure and beauty, bragging rights, or anything else they needed. But, in order to do that, he had to stop thinking about life's many uncertainties. He had to stop worrying about what the future might hold and focus on what he was doing now, right here, in this very moment.

He shook off the dark mood that threatened to settle over his spirit and went back to work with renewed energy. "Yeah, this is turning out nice. I'm really liking this a lot."

"I bet you say that to all the girls," Sophie said with a sigh.

Declan laughed. "I think you're probably right." He was rarely aware of having spoken out loud. It had always been that way. When he'd seen the first couple of episodes of *Inked in O-Town*, he'd been mortified and more than a little self-conscious. He'd tried to make himself stop, but the producers swore viewers loved it, so he'd learned to get over his discomfort. "But this is *really* pretty. I think you're going to be very happy with how it turns out."

"That's what I'm hoping."

"Count on it, *bébé*."

Sophie's artwork was lovely to start with of course. It was no wonder she was able to earn a living selling her sketches to tourists around Jackson Square. But Declan felt more than justified in taking some credit for how the final product was turning out. He hadn't been lying when he'd told her the scars weren't bad. Two long, somewhat jagged, vaguely pinkish scars had snaked across her chest, with a smaller, rounder mark positioned above. He'd positioned the drawings so that the petals of two full-blown poppies ran along the edges of the longer scars—so that they were incorporated into the picture rather than merely glossed over. And so that they added to the beauty he was creating and became part of it. The smaller scar became part of a bud, tightly furled, but raising its head above the others—a promise for the future. The *uncertain* future, as she'd insisted on reminding him. Something he couldn't think about right now.

When the flowers were finished, Declan stopped to study the effect. He had planned on adding more color to the background, maybe in contrasting shades of blue or even purple. It was a part of his trademark in a way, but it didn't feel quite right this time. Sophie's skin was luminous, but pale. The way the flowers stood out against it, vibrant and warm, might seem a little bit stark, yes, but in a way that caught the eye and made a statement. Anything else would only look garish and detract from the overall effect.

He put down his machine. Using a little soap, he wiped off the tattoo, still debating.

"You're making me nervous," Sophie said in a very small voice.

"No need for that. We're done." He nodded toward the mirror. "Take a look."

Sophie shook her head. "Not yet."

"Are you sure?" he asked, more than a little disappointed.

Sophie shrugged. "I'm just not ready."

"Okay, well..." Declan sighed. He supposed there was no reason she had to. It wasn't going anywhere, after all. Still, he was anxious for her reaction. "I guess you're not going to let me take pictures of it yet either, are you?"

"Please don't," Sophie begged. "You're not angry about that are you?"

"No, of course not." Pictures could wait too. Sooner or later, this tattoo *would* end up in his portfolio. It was too fucking gorgeous *not* to show off. But he could understand that she might not be ready for that yet. He could give her the time she needed to feel comfortable. This was Sophie, after all. Deep down, beneath the scars and the surgery, she was still the same girl she'd always been—exhibitionist streak and all.

"All right then," Declan said. "Why don't you sit up now? I want to get this plastic wrap on you. You probably won't be able to get it off by yourself, but I can help you with that later if you come back to my hotel with me. All right?"

Sophie frowned. "Aren't you busy tonight?"

"Yes, but only for a few more hours. Why don't you hang out here until I'm done? You go have a drink, enjoy the party, have some fun while I'm working, and then we'll go home. I know it will be late, but if you spend the night, we can walk down to Café du Monde in the morning for beignets." That was something else he knew about the girl she used to be—the girl he was sure she still was, somewhere deep inside—beignets were an irresistible lure.

Sophie hesitated for a moment longer, but finally she shook her head and smiled. "Well, if you're going to twist my arm..."

Declan grinned back at her. "You're damn right I am. Every chance I get."

Chapter Seven

It was well after midnight when they left the shop. Fireworks no longer lit up the sky over Jax Brewery, although a few random bottle rockets were still being set off from time to time. Bourbon Street was its usual crowded self. No surprise there; that party rarely ever stopped.

After Declan opened the door and let them into the suite, Sophie wandered over to the window. Music filtered in from the street three stories down. Part of her wished she was still out there, celebrating amid an anonymous throng of people. Part of her wished she even *felt* like celebrating. She didn't; she felt like crying. She was oddly unsettled. Getting tattooed tonight had been unexpectedly intense. Much more than she'd anticipated. Despite the occasional discomfort, she'd enjoyed being the focus of Declan's attention. She'd started out nervous, and she'd still been pretty nervous when he finished. Ever since she'd climbed off his table, however, she'd felt bereft. She wanted his hands on her again. Maybe he'd been right. Maybe she wasn't above making flimsy excuses to get what she wanted.

Declan came up behind her. As he lightly massaged her shoulders he said, "Why don't you come into the bathroom now? That plastic wrap's been on long enough—too long. I want to get it off and get you cleaned up and apply some fresh coconut oil."

Sophie leaned into his touch. "Do we have to?" she groaned.

"Yes. Of course we do. It's like I said, it shouldn't have been covered up as long as it has. Besides, aren't you even a little curious to see it?"

"Of course I am." Part of her was anyway. "I'm also nervous as fuck."

Declan gave her shoulders a shake. "See? That's exactly why I wanted you to take a look at it while we were back at the shop. If you'd already looked, the suspense would be over by now. But really, there's no reason to be nervous. It turned out great. Just don't panic if it's looking a little puffy or bruised by now. That'll go away in a few days."

Sophie nodded. "I know. You must've told me that at least a half dozen times tonight."

"I know, but I needed to make sure you were really listening. I want you to be excited about it. Somehow, I don't feel like you are."

"Of course I'm excited." Which was not quite true. She *had* been excited, but now that it was over, what she was feeling more than anything else was let down. It could just be her endorphins were depleted. Or it could be the fact that Declan would be leaving soon, and she'd have to learn to get along without him, all over again—without the comforting fantasy of "maybe someday".

The bathroom was just as beautiful and sophisticated and expensive as the rest of the suite, all black granite and white porcelain and bright lights. And a mirror that spanned an entire wall. It reminded Sophie of just how far apart she and Declan really were. She let him help her remove her shirt and didn't object when he kept her turned away from the mirror while he removed the plastic wrap and gently washed her clean. She didn't complain when he used his fingers to smooth a thin covering of oil all over her. All she could think about was her lousy sense of timing. She'd finally gotten used to his touch. She'd finally managed to get him to put his hands on her again—and it was bliss. But was it for the last time?

"Are you ready to see it now?"

Sophie sighed. "I guess so." She'd rather have done this alone. A little privacy would not have been out of place right now. But Declan was so anxious for her to see it, and she guessed she did kind of owe him that.

She held her breath as he turned her around. Then she gasped in surprise. She covered her mouth with both hands and just stared. The tattoo was exquisite. The poppies appeared to be three dimensional, living blossoms that had been frozen in time as they waved in an imaginary wind. Though she could still see the scars, they'd been...transformed somehow. They weren't hidden, but the placement of the flowers allowed them to virtually disappear into the picture in a way she'd never anticipated. They added to the picture. They contributed to the beauty he'd created. They were still there, but different. All the same, as she stared into the mirror, the only thought in her head was, *this is how it will always be from now on.*

"Well?"

Sophie nodded slowly. "It... I mean, yeah. It...it's just so..." Then she appalled herself by bursting into tears.

"Those are happy tears, I hope?"

Sophie gulped for breath. She wasn't even sure she could explain how she felt. "Yeah, sure, but it just... It just really hit me. There's really no going back now, is there?"

"What?" Declan stared at her in alarm. "Sophie, what are you saying?"

A shattered sob escaped her. "It's all so...*permanent.*" Yes, her body was prettier now. He'd done everything she'd asked him to, and more. She loved the flowers, loved the way they looked. She'd probably even love the way they made her feel—someday. But would it ever be enough?

Somehow, in the back of her mind, where all her most unrealistic hopes and dreams resided, she'd been clinging to the stupid belief that this was all a mistake. As if someday the doctors might change their minds and admit they'd been wrong. That somehow time would reverse, or she'd wake from this dream, or the joke would be over and she'd have her breasts back. It wasn't rational, not even a little, and she hadn't even realized she thought it until another equally permanent change had occurred and it had been forced into her awareness.

"Permanent?" Declan's voice was bleak.

Sophie nodded, still leaking tears. The tattoo was permanent. The loss of her breasts was equally so, and somehow that had all gotten mixed up together. "It's like I thought I could cancel out one change with another, but this is never going to go away, is it?"

Declan's face went white, only marginally less pale than the porcelain. He stumbled over to the tub and sat on the edge. "Jesus, Sophie. What the fuck? You hate it that much?"

"No." Sophie shook her head. "No, I love it. I do. They're beautiful. You did a fabulous job. It's just…I guess it hit me harder than I expected. Sometimes, I forget, you know?"

"Just tell me I did not just make things worse. Please."

That haunted look in Declan's eyes struck at her heart. On the one hand, she wanted to erase it. She wanted to find something to say that would comfort him. On the other hand, why was this about him? Why did she feel the need to apologize and, while she was on the subject, what was she actually apologizing for?

Was it so wrong that she wanted him to see her as he used to—as a sexy, desirable woman? Or that she wanted to be able to see herself that way? Not as a victim or an object of pity. And certainly not as a conveniently blank canvas for his ink.

He'd given her a beautiful tattoo, and she was grateful for that, but she didn't owe him anything more than gratitude. It wasn't her job to make him feel okay about things. Especially not this.

"I just wanted to do something that would make a difference," Declan said. "Something to make you feel better. I wanted to give you what you needed. Damn it, I knew this was a mistake."

"Yeah, well, maybe so. What do you want me to say? We don't always get what we want in life, do we? But here's something I *don't* need; I don't need you trying to fix me. I can't make myself feel better just so *you* can be happy. I'm not going to pretend for you. And I don't want you pretending either. So just don't worry about it, all right? I've been fine on my own this far. I see no reason why I can't just keep doing that."

"Except that maybe you won't have to now." Declan got up and walked over to where she stood. "I wasn't going to say anything yet, but I've been giving this a lot of thought. I've decided to leave the show. I'll talk to Christie and see if there's a chance they'll have me back at Midnight Ink. If not…well, fuck 'em. They're not the only shop in town."

Sophie's heart clenched. Hope blossomed within her— bright and bold as the poppies on her chest. She squelched it. No. He couldn't mean that. She could not have him *here* and not have *him*, it would be too hard to take. "What are you talking about?"

"I'm moving back to New Orleans. Who knows how long any of us have, you know? I guess I've already wasted enough time trying to figure shit out. I don't want to waste any more."

"Why would you do that?"

"To be with you of course. Unless you'd rather move to California instead?"

"Are you fucking kidding me?" Sophie glared. Sure, *now* he wanted her with him. As if. "Look, Dec, I am not some kind of social service project, something you can take on in an effort to ease your guilt. I'm not a charity case. I'm not a cause you can donate your time to. And...I know how much it's always killed you that you couldn't save your grandfather or your brother, but you can't make up for that now by trying to save me. I won't be your penance for that either. Hell, people can't even save themselves half the time, never mind someone else."

Declan shook his head. "This isn't about... Fuck. It's not about *any* of that. I love you. I want to spend time with you. Why is that hard to understand?"

"You love me? Oh, please. Since when? We haven't even talked to each other in five years!"

"I know that!" Declan reached out and took hold of her arms. "I know. I was an idiot, okay? But you can't put that all on me. You didn't call me either."

Sophie dropped her gaze. "Yeah, well, maybe you should take that as a hint and go back to California. Where you belong."

"What hint is that?" He bent at the knees, ducking his head to catch her gaze. "Sophie? What hint? Are you saying you don't care about me? That you haven't enjoyed these past two days? You don't want more? 'Cause I'm not buying it."

"Sure. It's been fun. But 'fun' is not the kind of thing you build a future on."

"I don't know why not. What else are you gonna build it on — misery? Anyway, who cares? I haven't asked you to marry me yet either, have I?"

"Good. Don't. Because I'm not saying yes!"

" Look, it's not that big a deal, all right? I can tattoo anywhere—here, there, it doesn't matter. But, for right now, I simply want to spend time with you more than I want to act. That's the bottom line. The tattoos I do on the show are great. They're interesting and all, but I think that's mostly because I'm doing things I wouldn't get to do otherwise. They get picked for me on the basis of whether or not they'd make for good TV. I kinda miss choosing my own tats, tattooing real people for reasons other than ratings."

"Yeah, but for how long?"

"How long what?"

Sophie sighed. "How long are you going to want to hang out with me, or do 'real' tattoos? You'll get bored, just like always. What then?"

"Wow. You know, I'd expect something like that from people who've only seen me on TV, but you *know* me. I'll get *bored*? Do you really think I'm that shallow?"

"Not shallow," Sophie said, disengaging herself from Declan's grasp. "Just... Please. I can't do this, okay? Of course I care about you—you know I do. But it's been only two days since you've been back, and already I want to be with you so bad it hurts."

Declan frowned. "Okay, why does that not sound like better news? Where's the problem?"

"The problem is that, once the novelty wears off, and you get over this quixotic kick you're on, you'll remember that there are other women out there—women who still have breasts. And they're just waiting for the chance to throw themselves at you."

"Damn it, Sophie. Is that what this is about?"

"Nah, I heard a rumor there's a pecan shortage. Aunt Sally's might have to stop selling pralines and I don't know how I can go on if that's the case. Of course that's what it's about. What did you think?"

"Jesus." Declan shook his head. "Okay, yeah, you know what? They were great. They were *really* nice. I miss them a lot. But, get it through your head already; I was not just in love with your breasts!"

"No. Get this through *your* head: *You* weren't in love at all! I don't know what you think you remember about us, Declan, but it's a lie. We were friends who liked to fuck each other. That's all we were. Everything else is just pity wrapped in nostalgia and covered in bullshit."

Declan blew out a frustrated breath. "You know what? This is ridiculous. I'm done talking." He grabbed his toiletry bag and searched through it until he found a condom.

"What are you doing with that?" Sophie asked.

"What do you think I'm gonna do with it? You're the one who said it: we're friends who like to fuck, right?"

Sophie's eyes widened in surprise. "You want to have sex? Now?"

"Yep. Any problems?"

Sophie thought for a moment. God, she could use the release. She shook her head."No, not really."

"Good."

"Yeah. Good." Very good, in fact. It hurt too much to think about the future, so she just wouldn't do it. But one more night of the best sex of her life—no strings, no expectations? That she could totally do. "Go for it, stud. Rock my world."

"Oh, believe me, that's just what I intend to do."

Sophie's pulse raced with excitement as Declan took hold of her hand and led her from the bathroom. Good. This was good. This was just what she needed. Something to take her mind off everything else.

But then Declan bypassed the bedroom and headed for the stairs that led to the suite's lower level. Sophie frowned. "Where are we going?"

"You'll see." He led her down the stairs and across the floor, not stopping until they'd reached the French doors leading to the balcony. Then he dropped her hand to unlatch the doors.

When he pushed them open, music and laughter and the buzz of voices assaulted Sophie's senses. The party was still going strong. "I *know* you don't think I'm going out there," she told him. For God's sake, she was practically naked! Her feet were bare, she'd left her shirt upstairs; all she was wearing were the yoga pants she'd put on that morning. "Not like this."

Declan shot her a wicked glance. "Why not? I think that's a great outfit." Then he reached for her hand once more and, before she could think to stop him, he drew her through the door.

"Fuck!" Sophie gasped as cool air flowed over her. Her tattooed skin felt vaguely sunburned. The soft breeze brushing against it felt heavenly. She yearned to lift her arms above her head and stretch, offering even more of herself to the night. But the awareness that she was barely dressed and out in public had her curling toward him instead, in an effort to hide her nakedness. "Jesus, Declan. This isn't funny. Quit blocking the door and let me get back inside before someone sees."

Declan folded his arms around her and held her close. "Relax, *bébé*," he murmured against her hair. "You're on Bourbon Street. Shirtless women are practically a fixture. Ain't a soul down there didn't come here tonight expecting to see something like this."

"Something like what, exactly?"

"You. Standing up here in all your glory. Screaming your pleasure to the night sky and starting the New Year with a bang. I think we're gonna put on a hell of a show for them, don't you?"

"Omigod." Heat blossomed inside Sophie as she thought about being so exposed. She did her best to ignore the delicious shiver that worked its way down her spine. "You're out of your fucking mind. And, just so you know? Those have got to be some of the worst lines ever. Get some new material, huh?   Also? Just for the record, I am *not* screaming."

"Not yet," Declan agreed as he moved them ever closer to the wrought iron railing. "And, here's the thing. If that's really what you want, you go right ahead and hold your tongue. There's so much going on down there right now that, as long as you stay quiet, I'm pretty sure no one'll even notice we're out here. It's your choice, but I'm not going to make it easy for you. I want to show you off—you and this gorgeous tattoo. I'm proud of my work, and I'm proud to be with you. And I want everyone down on Bourbon Street to see that. To see you. So I'm going to do everything I can to make you scream real, real loud."

"Oh, shit." Sophie sucked in a quick breath as Declan turned her toward the street. She couldn't believe they were out here like this—or, rather, that *she* was out here like this. He was still fully clothed—which only made her hotter. Were they really going to do this? How did he always talk her into these things? Part of her wanted to object, but then he placed her hands on the railing, spread them wide and pressed her forward, so that she was leaning out over the street. Her belly quivered as it made contact with the cold metal. She jumped, nearly squealing at the shock, but there was nowhere to go, no way to retreat. Her heart hammered, even harder than before as she looked down at the crowd milling below. Her pussy clenched. She could feel herself already dripping with arousal. In that instant, she knew she wasn't going anywhere. She couldn't have moved away from the rail or unclenched her hands if he'd asked her to.

But he didn't ask. Instead, he leaned into her from behind. His body, so hard against her own, accentuated the feeling of being trapped. She couldn't move. She didn't want to move, but even if she did…he'd stop her. He'd keep her here, *take* her here, where anyone might see her, where everyone *would* see her as soon as she opened her mouth and drew their attention upward.

It was all too much. "Oh, Declan, please…" She clamped her quivering thighs together, gulping for breath, unable to finish the sentence. "Please, please, please…" She wasn't even sure what she was asking for. "Why are you doing this?"

"Why are *we* doing this," Declan corrected as he lowered his head to nibble at her neck. "I'm not the only one out here, you know."

"Semantics," she groaned. "You know what I mean."

"I know a lot of things." Declan's hands caressed her, sliding up her arms and then down along her sides, his knuckles brushing over her ribs. "More than you give me credit for apparently."

He touched her everywhere — everywhere but where she was inked, everywhere but where she really needed his hands. He slid his arms around her waist and pulled her even more tightly against him.

"I know you, Sophie. I know you inside and out — what you like, what you crave, what your heart demands, even when you won't admit it. Are you really going to tell me you don't want this?"

Sophie whimpered at his touch. The words she wanted to speak wouldn't come. One night. One glorious, amazing, unforgettable, sinful night. Why shouldn't she have this?

"This isn't pity, Sophie Jane. You know that, right? Or any of those other things you said before. You're so beautiful when you're turned on like you are right now — it makes me hot just being near you. I'm not doing this for any reason other than that. I want you to see yourself like I see you. I want *everyone* to see you like this — so fucking sexy, with my ink all over you and my hands in your pants." He suited his actions to his words, pushing his fingers past the elastic of her waistband and then sliding both hands down the front of her pants. His fingers searched out and found her clit. "I want to tattoo you all over. Maybe you won't give me that. Maybe you won't give me anything else but this. I don't care. For tonight, you're mine. And I want everyone to know it."

"Oh, yes, there," Sophie moaned as she pushed into his touch. His fingers moved in slow strokes, over her clit, between her folds, growing slicker with every pass he made.

"I wish I could take these pants off you too," he whispered as he speared her core. "If I had you naked right now, do you know what I'd do? I'd spread your legs wide and hold you open. I'd finger you 'til you came. I'd let everyone watch as I did it. Is that what you want too? Tell me."

Sophie nodded, barely aware of what she was agreeing to. She pushed her hips forward again demandingly. "More." She doubted anyone could see what his hands were doing to her. Not yet. Not unless he really did remove her pants. She wouldn't put it past him.

At this point, she wouldn't put it past herself to let him either.

"God, Declan. How do you get to me like this?"

He was shameless, and she was enslaved — that had to be the answer. He'd put her under some damned voodoo curse. Or maybe she was the shameless one? After all, she was the one who was standing out here, bare-chested, leaning against the rail, writhing beneath his touch, already starting to come undone. Not caring at all about the crowd of people on the street below.

"Come for me," Declan urged as his fingers continued to press inside her, stretching and filling her, retreating then thrusting again, the heel of his hand pummeling her clit with that same demanding rhythm. "I want to be inside you when you do. I want your hungry little pussy chomping at my fingers, like you're about to eat me up."

His voice slid across her skin like sweet syrup, as seductive as the saxophone music rising from the street corner. She closed her eyes and turned away, trying to shut it all out. But he wouldn't let her. He pulled one hand from her pants and grasped the back of her head. Catching a handful of her too-short hair between his fingers, he tugged.

"Open your eyes," he ordered as he directed her attention to the street. "Look at them — all those people down there. Call to them. Let them see you. Let them see how gorgeous you are. Hot. Sexy. Mine."

Yes! Sophie whimpered as she bowed to the irresistible pressure of hard fingers inside her and in her hair, hard body behind her, hard railing in front, hard teeth at her neck. Everything hard, hard, hard. Unrelenting. Her back arched as she stretched toward the sky. A sob tore from her throat as she came, hands clenching on the metal rail, cunt clenching around Declan's hand. Twisting in ecstasy. She heard an enthusiastic cheer go up from the street below, just before she was swung around and whisked into the shadows.

"Need to fuck you," Declan growled as he carried her back inside, his voice a thick and desperate whisper her ear. "Need to be inside you, *bébé*. Now."

"Do it." She was still shuddering with aftershocks — sparks and remainders of an orgasm that continued to sizzle along all her nerves, just waiting for the chance to reignite. "Hurry. Do it. Do it now."

"Couch," he rasped out, as he headed across the room.

"Yes." Her hands clutched at him. She wanted, needed, more. So much more. More than he could possibly give her. She wanted to be face down on the cushions, his hand coming down on her ass with just enough strength behind it so that each slap would bring tears to her eyes. She wanted his knee sliding hard between her thighs, forcing them apart and then forcing them wider. She wanted all her fears and hesitations, all her worries for the future, to disappear, subsumed by his need for her. She wanted to feel the rough fabric of the upholstery as it abraded her chest, setting fire to her nipples with every thrust — and she wanted it hot enough, rough enough, mindless enough to obliterate the knowledge that it could never really be like that again.

Declan set Sophie back on her feet in front of the couch. They were both breathing hard by that point. Watching her shimmy out of her pants didn't help. She had him so distracted that he almost forgot take the condom out of his pocket. By the time he'd suited up, she was already reclining on the couch, watching him. He fell on top of her, careful to keep his weight on his arms as he pressed her back into the cushions. He kissed her again and again, tugging at her limbs and moving her around until she was beneath him.

Sophie wrapped one leg around his back — the other was braced on the floor. She looped her arms around his neck and pulled. "Come here," she begged. "Closer. I want to feel you all around me."

He shook his head. "Can't," he panted out between kisses. "Not tonight. That ink's too new." Oh, but he wanted to. Anything to close the distance between them, to knock down the walls she kept building to keep him out. Anything that didn't carry the risk of infection. He still didn't know enough about her condition to take that kind of chance.

Sophie groaned in frustration. "Damn it." Her teeth closed hard on her lower lip. "Need you."

"I know, *bébé*." He dragged the head of his cock along her slit several times, wishing he was bare, so he could really feel her wetness. Even with the condom she felt oh, so good, slick and soft and sexy. "I know. I've got you." But not if he didn't get inside her soon.

He took a shaky breath, hoping it would calm him because he was all set to go off like some kind of damn rocket. But the scent of her filled his nostrils, and his balls tightened. He'd swear he could taste her on the back of his tongue. He flexed his hips and thrust inside her quickly, needing to move. Her pussy clenched around him immediately, nearly ending things right then and there. It was the best kind of torture.

Another raw sob worked its way up Sophie's throat. "Yes. Oh God, yes. Like that. Just like that."

"Jesus, Sophie, you're killing me." He pulled out then surged into her once again, seating himself even deeper within her, setting up a steady rhythm that he hoped would drive them both insane. He was already there. She needed to go there again. Fast. "You were so fucking hot out there on that balcony. So fierce. So fearless." He'd loved seeing her like that, loved that she'd let him have that. It hadn't escaped his attention that she'd loved it too.

Best of all, she wasn't shielding herself from him anymore. Not physically. Maybe there *was* hope for them. She couldn't really think there was nothing more to them than this...could she?

He sat up and reached for her hands, untangling them from around his neck. Then he pinned them to the cushions on either side of her head. "I need you to tell me something." God, he loved how the slightest order still got to her. The small whimper she gave, the flush on her cheeks, the hitch in her breath, her glazed eyes—he loved it all. An excited little spasm rocked her pussy. His own breath skittered in his throat. His balls drew up tight. *Keep your shit together*, he ordered himself, *this is important*. He couldn't afford to mess up now.

"What?" Sophie groaned impatiently. "What now? What do you need me to say?"

"I need you to tell me that all that stuff you said earlier, in the bathroom, was bullshit. You *know* there's more between us than sex."

Sophie's expression turned anguished. "Declan, c'mon. Don't do this."

"I love you, Sophie." He bent his head and kissed her softly. "I do. I always did." He'd just been too stupid to admit it.

Sophie sighed. "Didn't always seem so."

"I know." He rocked against her, needing to feel the connection between them, needing to touch her deep inside. "And I'm sorry about that. I wasn't always good at figuring things out. But I've changed a lot in five years. I wish you could see that."

A sad smile touched her lips. "I've changed too—in case you hadn't noticed. It's kind of hard to miss."

"You still love me," he insisted, feeling less and less certain. "I know you do."

She shook her head. "What does it matter now?"

"It matters." Then he sealed her mouth with his, refusing to let another word come between them.

She sure didn't kiss him like it didn't matter — or like she didn't love him, either. He took comfort in that and rocked harder — long, deep strokes, just the way she liked it. Until she was thrashing beneath him, begging him for more. Until they were both on the edge where the smallest push would send them both over. "Let me in, Sophie," he whispered when he knew she was close. "Let me back in. Please. Stop shutting me out."

Her eyes flew open and locked with his — but only for an instant. He thought he read wonderment, questions, hopes, and dread there, but as fast as that, it was gone, and she was shuddering and convulsing in his arms. He thrust harder then, faster, needing her right there with him when he came. Not at a distance. Not on the phone. Not just a memory. But real. Here. Alive. His.

"Tell me," he rasped out. His need for her built with every stroke, every breath, every heartbeat, every thought — but it wasn't enough, never would be enough if he didn't have her heart. "Tell me."

"I love you," Sophie said on a sob. "I do, all right? I never stopped."

"Thank you." He gasped as he slammed inside her one last time, as his orgasm lit him up inside like fireworks over the Mississippi. "Thank you for that."

Love couldn't make everything better. It couldn't fix the world. But it made everything else so much easier to bear. It had taken him way too long to figure out that piece of wisdom.

"Do you know what I think I loved most about your breasts?" he asked a long time later. They were still curled up on his couch. He took comfort in that, comfort in the fact she hadn't bolted at the first opportunity. "I loved how responsive they were. I loved knowing I could make you feel so good just by touching them. But I think we've proven I can still make you feel good. We still have that, Sophie. Don't we?"

And, once again, Sophie was blinking back tears. His heart sank as she stared at him, her expression so very bleak. "You make everything sound so simple, but it's not. You make this sound so normal, but it's changed everything."

"It hasn't changed how I feel about you."

She sat up and pulled away from him. "It's changed how *I* feel about me. I know it's stupid, I know I should feel grateful, but sometimes I'm not. Sometimes... Hell, sometimes I feel like I don't even know who I am anymore."

Declan sat up as well. "Yeah," he said sadly. "I know. I get that." And he did, he really did.

Sophie scowled. "You don't know! Stop saying that. You can't possibly know what I'm going through. And the fact that you even think you can? The fact that you can sit there and act like it's no big deal? That just tells me how much you *don't know* about it."

"Of course it's a big deal. It's *huge*. And, I know, when that big a piece of yourself goes missing, it's hard to even make sense of who you are."

"Yes. Ex-exactly." Sophie blinked at him, obviously surprised by his insight.

A rueful smile curled Declan's lips. Did she really think him that clueless? And had he really thought he could do this without baring a big part of his own soul?

"You stay away from mirrors because they're too painful," he told her as the ghost of his own remembered heartbreak shafted through him. "Because the only thing you notice when you look in one, is everything that's missing, everything that's wrong. It's like you're suddenly trapped inside a new identity, and all you want is to have the old you back. Deep down inside, you know that's never going to happen. But it never stops haunting you. And you never stop hurting."

Understanding finally dawned in Sophie's eyes. She nodded, her expression softened now by sympathy. "Like when you lost your twin."

Declan cringed. "Did you know the first memorial tattoo I tried to get was his portrait? Yeah. I was so disconnected it didn't even occur to me that I was basically asking to have my own face tattooed over my heart. The artist had to point that out. I guess he thought I was some kind of crazy egomaniac or something. But it wasn't really *my* face, you know? I mean there were all those little differences between us, all the things that made Dev...Dev, and not me. But, suddenly, they no longer mattered. Hell, I was practically the only one left who even knew about them. And yet...I dunno. After awhile, it began to seem like those differences were the only things that defined me. Whenever I looked at my own face—in pictures, in the mirror, wherever—all I could see were the ways in which I wasn't him.

"Losing that connection... Well, it hurt so bad. I never wanted to feel that way again. So I did exactly what you're doing now. I tried to shut everybody out—especially anyone I cared about, anyone who tried to get too close, anyone I couldn't afford to lose."

He lifted her chin, forcing her to face him, needing to make his point, needing to be sure she understood. "And I'm going to tell you something right now, Sophie Jane, and I hope you're listening. That is *no* way to live."

"I know that." Sophie dropped her gaze. "I do. I know you're right, but…"

"I know I can't promise you forever. I wish that I could. But you and I both know that's not how the world works. Sooner or later, we all end up scarred. That's what life does to people. No one escapes. But life's not about playing it safe. It's about making memories and leaving marks. Because, when we're gone, that's pretty much all we'll leave behind us. Nothing but the marks we've made on the hearts and minds of the people we've loved. And on the people who've loved us back."

Sophie sniffed back tears. "When did you get to be so smart?"

He laughed at that. "Smart? Oh, darlin', that's not me. If I were smart, I'd have figured this shit out a *long* time ago." He gazed at her silently for a moment. Then he reached for her hand and held it tight. "Stay with me? Please? Let me be there for you."

Sophie nodded and smiled—a very watery smile, but he'd take it. "Okay."

"I'm not just talking about tonight, you know."

Sophie rested her head against his shoulder and sighed. "Yeah. I know."

Chapter Eight

One week later...

The shop was mostly deserted this early in the day. Shep studied the sketch that Declan had handed him, the curling pink ribbon that spelled out Sophie's name in script. Then he raised his head to glare accusingly at Declan. "What the fuck is this? You're saying you want me to tattoo a name on your chest?"

Declan rolled his eyes. "Oh good, you can read. Man, that's a relief. For a minute there, I thought I was going to have to walk you through this."

"Fuck you. Also: no way. I'm not doing it. What's with everyone wanting names all of a sudden? It's a curse. I think I told you that—what, ten years ago?"

"It was eight years ago. And so what? I still don't believe in curses."

"Yeah, well, it's your funeral then, ain't it?" He tossed the paper down on the counter. Folding his arms across his chest, he fixed Declan with a narrow-eyed gaze. "Why'd you come to me with this? Why not go to one of the others?"

Declan shrugged. "Why not you? I mean, aside from that truly god-awful tattoo you had to touch up the night of the party, you have a real talent when it comes to script-work."

"Hey! There was absolutely *nothing* wrong with that tat. She *moved*."

"I'm sure she did." Declan sighed. "All right, look, the thing is, this is important to me, okay? And all kidding aside, there's no one I'd trust with something like this more than you."

Shep shook his head. "All right, fine. You talked me into it. Just don't say I didn't warn you." He studied Declan for a moment then said, "So, I hear you're coming back for good."

"You heard right. Soon as I finish the current season, I'm quitting the show."

His agent hadn't been too happy with the news. And when Christie said he'd have to talk to the other artists before making a decision, Declan was sure he was screwed. He figured he'd burned his bridges a little too well when he'd left, and his TV career wasn't likely to help. He'd been shocked when Christie had welcomed him back into the Midnight Ink fold, even more so when he mentioned that the vote had been unanimous. He'd been shocked, humbled, grateful, touched—not that he was ever going to admit to any of that! He had a reputation as a smart-ass to uphold after all.

"Just so you know, it's gonna suck having you around again all the time."

Declan smirked. "Uh-huh. Sucks to be you, you mean. Now, can we get this tat started? And don't mess it up, all right?"

"Oh, kiss my ass. I'll do my job, you do yours. Just don't move."

"Wouldn't dream of it. I'm here to stay."

Bonus short story!

Blame It on the Voodoo

By PG Forte

What's a little black magic among friends? Vampire Rene Boudreaux is more than a little annoyed. It seems sexy voodoo queen Zirondelle Doucette has got him under her spell. Can Zee convince Rene that the only real magic is love? Or will he continue to blame it on the voodoo?

"It's getting to where you can't swing a dead chicken around here anymore without it smacking into one damn psychic or another."

Zirondelle Doucette couldn't help the grin that spread across her face as she listened to her Aunt Serafina's complaints. Her aunt stood at the window of their family's shop, staring out at the street, and Zee didn't have to guess too hard to figure out the cause for her discontent. Another "damn" psychic had recently put out her shingle in the previously vacant storefront directly across from their own.

"And if it's not a psychic it's a card reader," the other woman continued, grumbling crossly. "Or a palm reader. Or tea-leaf reader—"

"Or a purveyor of Voodoo essentials?" Zee suggested, holding up the little gris-gris bag she'd just finished assembling.

Serafina turned her head to glare at her niece. "Don't sass me, Zee. You know exactly what I'm talking about."

"Yes, Ma'am, I do." Ducking her head, Zee started in on the next charm. She knew it wasn't psychics *per se* with whom her aunt had a problem. Serafina was a tolerant soul, not the kind who'd ever take a stand against anyone else's religion or spellcraft or spiritual beliefs. It was the idea of all those make-believe mystics making a mockery of their family's calling that was trying the older woman's temper, and not without cause. The Doucette family had owned and operated their establishment in the self-same Royal Street location for several generations, dealing in authentic rituals, in candles and jujus, talismans and spells. It was hard not to take it personally when your way of life was turned into a kind of circus act by greedy imposters. But as Zee and her aunt both knew, the charlatans did in fact have a place and a purpose in the grand scheme of things.

Oh, how the tourists loved them. They ate up their acts and purchased their trinkets as eagerly as they did the beignets at the Café du Monde. Or jazz on Frenchmen Street. Or hurricanes in Pat O's Courtyard. It was all part of the Crescent City mystique, like Po' Boys and crawfish, pralines and beads. In an odd way, they kept things safe. They kept the merely curious from straying into dangerous territory.

"Oh, Lawd." Aunt Serafina's sudden gasp caught Zee's attention. She glanced up in surprise.

"Auntie, what's wrong?"

"It's him." Serafina scurried back behind the counter where her niece was working, babbling nonsensically. "He's back. He's coming this way. What should we do? What does he want this time?"

"Do about what?" Zee asked, feeling mystified and mildly exasperated. "Who's back?" She loved Serafina; truly she did. Her aunt had taken Zee in after her parents passed, without question or hesitation—the only member of their somewhat eccentric family who seemed to have any idea about what to do with a bewildered little girl who'd suddenly been orphaned. Zee would never forget the older woman's kindness but, all the same, there were times, like now, when dealing with her aunt seriously tried Zee's patience.

The Doucette family had a certain reputation; they were known for being fierce and fearless. They prided themselves on it, in fact. But Serafina had always been unusually timid for a Doucette. Right now, her pale eyes, also unusual in a Doucette, were wide with fear, the pupils dilated; her voice was but a whisper. "Monsieur Boudreaux."

Boudreaux. The name itself meant very little. It was as common as dishwater around those parts. But between the look on her aunt's face and the singing certainty in her own heart, Zee knew exactly which Monsieur Boudreaux Serafina meant. She meant Rene Alcide Boudreaux. Zirondelle's Monsieur Boudreaux. Dominant. Vampire. Master.

But not *her* master. No, not yet.

As the door to the shop swung open, Zee trembled inside. She couldn't even raise her eyes to gaze upon the shadow that she knew must be filling the entryway. Odd, considering that shadow contained the very thing for which she'd been longing.

"Good evening, Madame Doucette, Mademoiselle." Rene glided into the shop with his usual preternatural grace. He had a way of moving that Zee found mesmerizing. And his voice! That subtle growl, as dark and seductive as midnight, left Zee wanting to fall to her knees at his feet and declare her submission right then and there. She dared not, however. Not with her aunt looking on. Not when she hadn't yet been granted the right.

"Monsieur Boudreaux." Serafina's voice shook a little as she returned his greeting. "What a surprise. We weren't expecting you."

"Weren't you?"

"Well, yes. I mean…no! It—it's so soon after Monsieur's last visit."

That was sadly true, Zee reflected. Although he'd once been a regular customer, stopping by every few weeks, things had changed in the last decade. Nowadays it was not unusual for a year or more to pass between encounters. Rene's last visit to the shop had been three months ago. The occasion was burned into Zee's memory because it was then she decided that enough was enough. It was time to take matters into her own hands, to go after what she wanted, to stop waiting, hoping or dreaming that Rene might someday recall her existence. She could be dead by the time that happened!

"Indeed," Rene agreed. "However, I'm sure you'll appreciate that circumstances have made it necessary that I return sooner rather than later. I'm here because of the spell that's been placed upon me — the curse, if you will."

"A curse!" Serafina gasped in alarm. "Oh, surely Monsieur is mistaken."

"I assure you, Madame, the mistake is not mine. It would, in fact, be rather impossible for me to be mistaken about such a thing. You see, if there's one thing we vampires are very familiar with, it's curses. Centuries of people wishing one dead or ill tends to naturally have that effect."

"But...who would dare do such a thing?"

Zee glanced at her aunt in surprise. *Any number of people,* she was tempted to reply. Was that not the very reason Rene had been coming to them all these years? He'd been their most loyal customer since practically the first day they'd opened for business. The Doucettes had grown rich selling charms and protection spells to people like Rene Boudreaux. Even if she privately shared her aunt's skepticism, surely it was bad business to mention the fact!

Rene's brow furrowed. He stared searchingly at Serafina for several seconds, then inclined his head. "I apologize. I'm sorry to have alarmed you, Madame. I can see now that you had nothing to do with the difficulties I've been experiencing. Might I have a word with your niece? In private?"

"Wi-with Zee?" Serafina stammered. "In p-private?"

Zee could tell her aunt was gathering her courage to refuse. She was touched by Serafina's protective instincts, but right now those instincts were as unnecessary as they were unwelcome.

"Why, Monsieur, I...I hardly th-think that's necessary."

"It's all right, Auntie," Zee said quickly. "Why don't you go into the backroom and brew up one of your tisanes. I'm sure it will help calm your nerves."

Serafina gazed piteously at her. "Zee..."

"It's all right," she repeated, a little more firmly. "Really." She patted her aunt's arm and smiled reassuringly. It was more than all right, actually. A chance to be alone with her beloved Rene? That was cause for celebration! But even so, as her aunt, with a sad little nod and a reluctant backward glance, retreated from the room, Zee found a little of her confidence deserting her. Her gaze dropped once more. The rush of blood was so loud in her ears she could not even hear Rene's footsteps on the floorboards. Oh, but she felt his approach just the same. His powerful presence pervaded the atmosphere. She was paralyzed by it, enraptured, entranced.

"Zirondelle. Look at me."

Her name on his lips was the sweetest caress. His words were a command she could not disobey. She glanced up immediately, gaze locking with his piercing blue eyes. "Yes?"

"I know it's you."

"Wh-what? Me?" She drew in a shaky breath. "You do?" Well. It was only about time, wasn't it? After all, she'd known it was *him* for most of her life. He was her destiny, her fate, the other half of her soul.

"Yes. I know it's you who's cast this spell upon me."

Zee's heart sank. Was that all he was talking about? Disappointment fueled her defiance. She tossed her head and demanded, "And? What if it was?"

"Then you will remove it. At once."

"What if I won't?"

His eyes widened. "You would dare defy me?"

Would she? The thought shook her and, for just a moment, she considered backing down. She didn't want him angry with her, after all. Even if she weren't madly in love with the man, she still would never want to make an enemy of him—no one with any sense at all would want that! On the other hand, desperation was a powerful goad. At this point, she was willing to go pretty far to attract his attention. And if this was what it took, so be it.

Besides, foolish or not, she just could not bring herself to fear him all that much. She'd known him all her life. This was the same Rene Boudreaux who was so kind to her as a child, who'd comforted her as no one else could have following her parents' tragic and untimely deaths.

It was he who'd found her, hiding beneath a table in the funeral home, paging feverishly through a book of spells she'd taken from her grandmother's house, looking for something—anything—that might bring them back. Curses were not the only things with which vampires were familiar. They knew death and loss better than anyone else. When Rene had promised her she would not die from a broken heart, when he insisted no spell was necessary, that her parents had not really gone anywhere, that those we truly love will continue to live on eternally, enshrined in our hearts forever, Zee believed him.

Now, remembering that day, remembering all his kindness—both then and after—a smile curved her lips. "Why not? I think I would. After all, I know you'd never hurt me." Not unless she wanted him to.

Rene sighed. "This is insupportable." He shook his head wearily and asked, "What is it you want from me, child?"

"Not very much." Other than for him to stop thinking of her as a child and recognize her finally as a woman, one who knew her own heart and was willing to be whatever he wanted or needed her to be. "Just one night. One night with you."

"What's that?" Rene stared at her in alarm. "No. Impossible. You don't know what you're asking for."

"I don't?" She smiled a little and teasingly said, "Well, if that's the case, it's all the more reason, isn't it?"

No matter what Rene might assume, Zee really didn't think it was possible that there was anything she didn't know about the man. Her family had always kept very meticulous records on the people they did business with—as a form of insurance, if nothing else—and Zee had studied those records in depth. She knew his history, his pain and his sorrow. She knew his tastes and predilections. She knew all about his illicit affair with her great-great-great-aunt Adeline.

The Doucettes were not long-lived in general, but Adeline had died even younger than was usual for one of their clan, consumed by her passion for Rene Boudreaux, or so the story went. Though most of the family seemed to regard Adeline's sad fate as a cautionary tale—a perfect example of why, especially when it came to matters of the heart, one should steer clear of vampires in general and Rene Boudreaux in particular—Zee had never found the story off-putting. Whatever had happened to Adeline, and Zee was not convinced anyone knew the full story there, she was sure it had not been Rene's fault. At least not entirely.

And even if it had been, so what? There were certainly worse ways to meet one's end.

It was possible Rene didn't know about the file of information her family had amassed about him, although Zee found it hard to imagine he could be so naïve that he didn't at least suspect they had one. Still, he couldn't believe her completely ignorant of his ways. He must have noticed the way she'd been dogging his footsteps these past months, yearning, learning, studying his every move. Why, she'd visited the sex club he owned and operated on Bourbon Street so frequently that she was now on a first-name basis with the bouncers and bartenders. She'd seen him in full Dom mode, dressed in black leather that fit him like a second skin and added further fuel to her fantasies. She'd watched while he demonstrated proper flogging techniques. She'd listened as he explained how best to discipline an unruly sub. She'd dreamed of one day experiencing all of that for herself.

In short, she'd done her homework. She knew exactly what she was risking, exactly what she was asking for as she repeated her request. "One night. With you. In your dungeon."

A shudder ran through his frame. It may have been nothing more than a sudden chill or a ghost walking over his grave, as the saying goes, but Zee didn't want to believe that was the case. She wanted to believe it was a sudden rush of heat that was affecting him. A desperate need to dominate her. An overwhelming desire to have her naked, bound and totally at his mercy.

Open, vulnerable, his—wasn't that exactly what she wanted too? Her heart soared with the sudden hope that tonight might see both their goals realized.

His stern gaze held hers for a moment longer. "And then you'll release me from your spell?"

Once again disappointment stabbed at her heart. Once again she ducked her head and sighed. "Then I will do whatever you ask of me."

"Very well." Rene's voice sounded unexpectedly grim. "If that's the way it has to be. Go and tell your aunt you're leaving. And be quick about it. I don't like to be kept waiting."

Zee nodded, not trusting herself to answer. Not trusting herself to say *yes* without adding *Master*. It was still too soon for that.

Out in the street, warm night air caressed Rene's skin and teased his tastebuds with a mélange of scents and flavors—bourbon, brown sugar, crawfish boil, dark coffee, rum—trivial things for which he had no longer any use. Ah, but there had been a time, he could still remember it, when he'd found them enjoyable, when such simple pleasures had the power to satisfy all his appetites. The sultry-sweet sound of a sax floated on the breeze and up ahead he could see a young couple dancing together on the banquette. They look happy, innocent, in love; for a moment, he envied them that. Once, he had been just like them—before time and loss had twisted his soul. The pleasures he craved now were darker, hotter, more intoxicating and far more dangerous. Like the pleasure of mastering Zirondelle Doucette.

To have her within his control, at his command, her body and mind—his to explore, to discover, to pleasure again and again. How he'd love to have the training of her. Oh, the things he could show her! He'd be the first to witness her response, the first to ever have her in any of a dozen different ways.

Such a thing was impossible, of course. He should put it from his mind. But he couldn't help thinking about it all the same. In fact, try as he might, these past few weeks that had been *all* he could think about. Given the way she'd been flitting about on the edges of his existence all that time, invading his thoughts, never leaving him a minute's peace, she deserved the flogging he had every intention of administering tonight. Why, she'd even haunted his dreams.

It had to be a spell. Had to be. And after all the money he'd given her family over the years! All the charms he'd purchased — all to ensure that just such a thing as this never occurred again. He should demand a refund. Not that it would do him any good.

He should have recognized right from the start what was happening to him. He should have confronted Zirondelle the first night she visited his club and ordered her then to keep her distance. Or, better yet, he should have simply left town years ago — back when he'd first realized that the uncommonly pretty child he'd grown so fond of, who he'd so enjoyed visiting and spending time with, was fast becoming an impossibly beautiful woman. One whose appeal he would never be able to resist.

He could still recall, even after nearly a decade, the shock he'd felt the day he'd first caught sight of that look in her eyes. Combining the innocent trust of a child with the needs of a woman and the devotion of a true submissive, it shook him to his soul. Even then, as inchoate as it was, it left him stunned, hungry, craving her with a desperation he had not felt in over a century.

It was wrong to feel the way he did about so young a girl, and he certainly had never acted on those feelings! But they tormented him all the same.

When one's desires can lead only to the destruction of precisely that which one holds most dear, it's best to distance oneself. Or, better yet, not to love at all. So he'd told himself, over and over again. And so he'd kept his distance, fearing for Zirondelle's wellbeing, hoping in time his own madness would pass. And mostly succeeding, until her innocent spell had ensnared him. Until her childish capriciousness had caused her to stray into dangerous territory, landing them both in bigger trouble than she knew.

Now, as she joined him on the banquette, looking far too happy, excited and pleased with herself, looking like everything he wanted—and everything he knew he shouldn't allow himself to have—he wondered how it had come to this. Perhaps he'd been fooling himself all along. Perhaps all his experience had taught him nothing. Perhaps it was his fate to always repeat the same mistakes. For her sake, he hoped to God that was not the case.

All the same, as he placed a hand on her back to guide her over to where his car was parked, he couldn't help wondering if he wasn't just leading them both down the path of irresistible temptation.

It's Voodoo. It has to be. That's the only acceptable explanation.

A spell, after all, could be lifted. A curse could be removed. Their effects would dissipate like the evening mist and all would be as it had been before. Anything else was simply too hopeless to contemplate.

Rene unlocked his car. "Get in," he said as he held the passenger door open.

Zirondelle glanced at the car in surprise. "We're driving? Why? Where are we going?"

It seemed an odd time for her to start raising objections—not that she shouldn't object to what he had planned for her. Not that he shouldn't be happy that she'd finally come to her senses. And he was happy. Perfectly so. "Where do you think we're going? I'm taking you back to my house. Isn't that what you wanted?"

"Oh." Her tongue emerged to nervously lick at her plush, pink lips. She gazed at him uncertainly. "Yes. I-I guess."

Rene tried hard not to think about how soft and delicious those luscious lips would feel pressed against his own, how easily they'd part for his tongue, how urgently he longed to taste them. He raised an eyebrow. "Have you changed your mind? It's not too late for that, you know. Release me now and promise never to do such a thing again and we'll both forget it ever happened."

Immediately, Zirondelle's chin rose. "No," she said quickly. "Who said anything about changing my mind? We have a deal. Let's go." Suiting her actions to her words, she slipped quickly into the seat. She pulled the door shut and stared defiantly at him through the window.

Rene sighed wearily. As he rounded the front of the car, he tried hard to ignore the treacherous feeling of relief that was filling his heart. There was nothing to feel relieved about. Nothing at all.

The low-slung sports car was sleek and elegant and somewhat understated, much like the man to whom it belonged, Zee couldn't help but reflect. But that was only on the outside. Beneath the unassuming surfaces, the gleaming midnight blue paint and butter-soft, oyster-gray leather, the genteel manners and studied calm, they both thrummed with power.

He's taking me home! Her heart beat faster at the thought of their tryst taking place in such an intimate setting. It was all she could do to keep from grinning like an idiot. She hadn't dreamed she would be this lucky—especially not tonight! All the same, she couldn't help feeling just a little intimidated, too. So much for being up-to-date on her information. She'd been assuming they would go to his club. She had no idea he even had a dungeon in his house. Not even in Adeline's diary had there been any mention of such a thing.

She was still fairly certain he lived alone, however. So, unlike at the club, there would be no witnesses to what went on tonight. If things went bad, if they took a turn for the ugly, there'd be no one to hear her scream, no one at all to intervene.

"So, why the sudden interest?" Rene broke the silence to ask.

"Who said it's sudden?" Zee replied, eyeing him cautiously. It was true they'd seen far too little of each other in the past ten years, but did he really not know how she long she'd yearned for him?

"Oh?" Rene's jaw clenched. His hands tightened on the steering wheel. "What are you saying then? You've experimented with such activities before? When? Where? With who?"

"What?" Zee frowned. "Wait. Are you talking about…BDSM?"

"Yes, of course. For want of a better term," Rene replied. "It's not one I favor. What else did you think we were talking about?"

"Oh, I don't know." Zee quickly brushed the question aside. "Nothing. It's not important." She'd thought they were talking about him, about them, about the heart and source of her real interest. But that, she supposed, was simply too much to hope for. "No, I haven't experimented very much at all." There was no one else she wanted to do this with, no one else she trusted. No one else she wished to surrender to.

"Then why have you been pushing so hard? Is it all just idle curiosity? Why choose me?"

Ah, there was a question. Zee felt her lips curve into a small smile. If only she knew the answer to it. But who could ever say why they'd fallen in love? Love wasn't math or science, something you could quantify or dissect. Love was a mystery. It was magical, mystical and very much like the Voodoo spell he claimed to be under. "It's not just curiosity. I told you: I've been interested for a while. And why not you? Why not the best?"

"Hmph." Was that a pleased smile teasing the corners of Rene's lips? Zee wasn't sure, but she thought it might be. "Well," he replied at last, grudgingly. "I certainly can't fault your logic there."

It was a short drive to the Garden District where Rene's home was located. The house was well maintained, but Zee would not have been at all surprised to learn that the early 19th century mansion looked just the same now as it had when it was first constructed. Only the mature landscaping surrounding the structure gave witness to the march of time.

The room he eventually ushered her into was located at the back of the house and here, finally, was something different! Given its location, the room had probably originally been meant to function as a morning room. A vampire would have no earthly use for such things, of course, so why not turn it into something vastly more entertaining, like a dungeon? She chided herself for having imagined something subterranean. This was New Orleans after all, where even burials took place above ground.

As she glanced around, taking in her surroundings, Zee couldn't suppress a tiny shiver of hunger, of longing…and yes, okay, perhaps a little bit of fear. The room was dark, its windows draped and shuttered, its walls painted a deep burgundy over oak wainscoting. It was intimate without being claustrophobic, warm and…welcoming somehow. She supposed that was due to the furnishings. Mostly well-oiled leather and wood, there was something substantial and vaguely comforting about them. They gave one the impression of having aged and mellowed with time. Of being solid and trustworthy. Only the shiny steel clamps and restraints, gleaming dully in the dim light, struck a modern and somewhat sinister note.

Rene escorted her to a small, curtained changing area and left her there with the demand she strip and await his return. She shed her clothes slowly, hampered in part by the surprising shakiness of her fingers.

"Are you sure this is what you want, Zee?" her aunt had asked when Zee had told her where she was going.

She'd nodded and smiled, feeling the same sense of certainty she was feeling now. "Yes, Auntie. I've never been more sure about anything."

All her life it had been Rene. Even as a young girl she'd dreamed of him. Every fantasy she'd ever had had centered around him. She'd had boyfriends, of course, one or two of whom she'd even imagined herself in love with. But no one had ever come close to touching that place in her heart that belonged only to Rene. Eventually she'd been forced to the realization that no one ever would.

As she grew older, her dreams had changed, but not very much. What mostly changed was that now she had a name for her desires; she had a context for her feelings. She knew exactly what she wanted. She wanted to submit to him. To surrender her heart to his care. To place her body in his capable hands. To hold nothing back and give him everything he demanded. And if it happened that those demands included a touch of pain, so much the better. That was something else she'd learned about herself, how the pain transmuted into pleasure, how it made love better, sweeter, hotter. How she longed for it.

Just a touch of pain, however. A hint—no more. Unrelieved suffering, either mental or physical, was no one's desire. She was equally certain of that.

Zee had read the letters Rene had written to Adeline. She'd wept at his pain when he'd begged his lover to let him change her in a last-ditch effort to save her life after she'd fallen so gravely ill. She'd wept even harder at the letter written after Adeline had refused him, after she'd chosen death for herself and doomed Rene to centuries of tormented loneliness. That sort of pain was not something she would have wished on anyone, let alone someone as dear to her as Rene.

If it had been Zee in Adeline's place, their story would have had a far different ending. She would have sacrificed anything to be with him. So what if the life of a vampire was dark and unnatural, as Adeline had claimed? It was the only life he had to offer his lover. How could she reject it out of hand? How could she choose to abandon him to his lonely fate, when she might have shared it with him?

Still, Zee couldn't help but be grateful for Adeline's decision. After all, it had opened a door for her. It had given Zee the chance to aspire to something even better than she would have had otherwise. Maybe she couldn't unbreak Rene's heart, but she could still hope to be the woman who brought that organ back to life, who healed his heart—just as once he'd healed hers.

The hiss of the curtains being whisked brusquely aside was the only warning she had. She turned and promptly lost her breath. There he was. Standing right in front of her. The look on his face and in his eyes was one she'd never seen there before, stern and autocratic, even more intense than when he'd been at his club. He was wearing leather pants, so thin and soft they molded to his thighs, and a leather vest that left his arms and most of his chest bare. Those she'd seen before, of course, but never like this, never close enough to touch. Now more than ever, the sight left her weak in the knees. Perhaps it was knowing that he wore them for her, but once again she felt the compulsion to fall at his feet. This time, she gave into it—or she would have, if he hadn't stopped her.

"No." Even as she started to lower herself, he grabbed her by the arm, keeping her erect. There was an unrestrained hoarseness to his voice when he spoke. "Not yet. Not here. Go stand over there. In the light."

She nodded her head once, feeling lighter than air and powerful beyond belief. The hand with which he held her arm vibrated, as though he could barely maintain his control. The knowledge she could affect him to this extent thrilled her. When he released her, she walked proudly over to the place he'd indicated, beneath the ornate brass and crystal ceiling fixture and stood there waiting.

The sway of Zirondelle's hips riveted Rene's attention as he slowly followed her across the room. He circled her deliberately, struggling for control while instinct urged him to fall upon her naked form and feast at her throat. She reminded him so much of Adeline. Why had he never realized that before? Why was she choosing to taunt him in this manner? Perhaps someone else had bespelled them both? If that was so, it was cruel beyond belief.

He'd loved Adeline with all his heart. Despite what her family had believed, he would have willingly sold his soul to save her. He'd have given anything to keep her from harm. In the end, however, he had nothing of any value to offer her. At least, nothing she was willing to accept. Why was that? Why had she rebuffed his offer? He'd spent years, decades, asking himself those same questions, never finding any answers. Was it somehow his fault? Had he frightened her that much? Had she spied the darkness within him and chosen death instead? Maybe he had held on too tightly. Maybe she had been just that desperate to escape from him.

If he fell now for Zirondelle, would the same thing happen again? Could he save either one of them? Or was it already too late to prevent another disaster?

"I don't know why you insisted on coming here tonight," he growled, still struggling for control. "And I still think this is a mistake. But, so be it. From here on in, you're mine. Mine to do with as I see fit. You will do as I say. You will take what you're given. And I hope for your sake you realize what you've let yourself in for."

"I do," she said, boldly raising her eyes to meet his gaze.

"Silence!" Rene barked in response. "Did I say you could speak? I thought you said you were familiar with how this works. You are to say nothing unless you are asked a direct question. And then you will answer only 'yes, Master' or 'thank you, Master,' as the situation dictates. And that is all you will say. Is that understood?"

Zirondelle released a shaky sigh. A tremulous smile curved her lips as she answered, *"Yes, Master."*

Rene ground his teeth. It was obscene the way her voice caressed the words and she looked altogether too happy for someone who he'd just had to reprimand, entirely too pleased with herself. Where was the fear? Where was the remorse? Where was the submission?

"Why are you doing this?" he snapped. "You're obviously not serious about any of it. Is it all a game to you? Casting spells, playing childish pranks—have you no idea how much danger you've placed us both in with your foolishness?"

The smile slid away from Zirondelle's face. She gazed at him darkly, silently. Her eyes grew hooded, speculative, remote.

Rene's temper continued to disintegrate. "Answer me, damn it!" he ordered, abandoning the very protocol he'd just laid out for her. "Tell me what you're up to."

"It's not a game. And I'm not a child any longer. And I never cast any stupid spell. So if you're really expecting me to release you when we're done here, you're out of luck. I'm doing this because I love you. How can you not know that?"

"No." Rene took a step back, recoiling from her words as he would from sunlight—both had the power to destroy him. "Stop it. Don't say things you don't mean."

"But I do mean it," Zirondelle insisted. "I've *always* loved you, for as long as I can remember. Tonight, I saw a chance to spend some time with you, to show you how I feel, to force you to notice me, so I took it."

"So it's an act? Is that what you're saying? All your supposed interest is nothing more than a ploy to garner my attention?" Rene fought a sudden urge to shake her 'til her teeth rattled. "Is that why you've never tried any of this before?" Why was he so surprised? She certainly wasn't the first woman who'd pretended to share his interests—only to realize too late all that it entailed. Only to recant her words, her promises after he'd given her his heart.

Zirondelle shook her head. "Of course not. That would be stupid. Who would do something like that? It's what I crave too. But…only with *you*. You're what I want. You're *all* I want. And this is part of what you are."

"Silence," Rene growled. Hope and fear warred within him and he couldn't listen to any more of this. It was time to test her resolve, to challenge her brave words. It was time to see for himself just what it was she wanted.

Zee watched as Rene stalked over to the large cabinet that she'd assumed housed his toys. He opened the door, grabbed something from the shelf and strode back to where she stood waiting. Her eyes widened at the sight of the ball-gag clenched in his fist. Why bother explaining what she was and wasn't to say if she wasn't to be allowed to say anything at all?

"Open," Rene ordered.

Zee opened her mouth reluctantly and allowed him to fit the gag snugly into place. Her head swam. The rubber tasted bitter but she could not deny the small thrill that shot through her as it filled her mouth. Her nipples tightened. Her pussy pulsed with need. Who knew such a small thing could turn her on so quickly?

Still, as Rene took her arm and led her over to the large cross that dominated one whole corner of the room, she couldn't help but worry. Her heart pounded fiercely. They hadn't even discussed safewords — not that words would do her any good at the moment, of course. But shouldn't they at least have established some sort of signal? Wasn't that a basic requirement? Safe. Sane. Consensual. She recited the words in her head, wondering how many of them actually applied to her current situation. Did any of them?

If his plan was to test her trust in him, he was doing a fabulous job!

Her nerves spiked higher after he'd fastened her in place and left her. She slowed her breathing as best she could and tried hard not to hyperventilate. Passing out before they'd even gotten started was no way to prove her sincerity. His footsteps receded across the room and she could only wait and wonder what implement of destruction he was planning to use on her. She didn't have long to wait. All those trips to his club had not been for nothing. She recognized the swishing sounds she heard behind her. So. He'd gone for the flogger. She supposed it could be worse.

As the first stroke landed across her upper back, however, she realized she'd seriously misjudged him. It wasn't just better than worse, it was...perfect. A quick splash of heat. A slow, spreading burn. Lightning fast strikes that brought tears to her eyes, that stung her flesh as though she'd sat too close to the fire on a cold winter's night.

The constant barrage locked down her thoughts, leaving her mind wide open to sensation. And then, just when she feared it might all become too much...it stopped.

Rene pressed against her from behind and Zee moaned weakly. Her head was spinning and everywhere his body made contact with hers, her skin sizzled. She was surprised to realize she was trembling on the brink of orgasm.

"Well?" he asked, his lips close to her ear. "Is this what you want?"

And just like that, Zee tumbled over the edge. She moaned and nodded, sagging against him as the tremors seized her. *Yes. Oh, yes. Oh, God, yes.* This was definitely what she'd wanted. How could he doubt it?

Rene was breathing heavily as he released her — first her ankles and then her wrists — keeping one hand anchored at her waist to steady her. Carefully, he turned her to face him. She leaned against him, still shaky, still not quite trusting her legs to hold her up. He tenderly removed the ball-gag from her mouth and stared down at her, his eyes dark as he studied her face.

"Just so you know," he said at last, "I've always loved you as well."

Then, before Zee had even an instant to process his words, he kissed her. Gasping slightly in surprise, she wound her arms around his neck and held on tight. As he claimed her mouth, she did the same to his, pressing herself against him, delighting in the feel of his strong hands caressing her skin, soothing away the heat.

When he finally let her go she glanced up at him. "You can't blame this on the Voodoo, you know," she told him, needing to get that straight. "There was no spell. No curse. No nothing. Not on my end. If you're really in love with me, that's all on you. You did that to yourself."

"Silence." Heat raced across her skin once again as his hand made contact with her ass. She squeaked in surprise. "Did I give you permission to speak?"

Zee bit her lip. She held his gaze an instant longer, then lowered her eyes and softly whispered, "No, Master."

Rene sighed. Gently, he brushed her hair back behind her ears. "We'll talk about that later."

Zee couldn't be sure, but she thought she heard the hint of a chuckle in his voice.

"In the meantime, I can see I have my work cut out for me. There's still so much you have to learn, so much I'll have to teach you. Why, I'll probably have to spend years training you, an entire lifetime in all likelihood. Won't I?"

His voice trembled just a little on those last two words. The doubt and the longing and the slight uncertainty in his tone filled Zee's heart with warmth. Try as she might, she couldn't keep from smiling as she met his gaze once more and happily answered, "Yes, Master."

This story was originally published as part of

Nine Nights in New Orleans

A collection of short stories written by

the *Nine Naughty Novelists*

More about Nine Nights in New Orleans:

Once upon a time, there were nine naughty novelists. Through the magic of the Internet, they came together for blog hijinks, friendship, and more. They bonded over their shared love of wine, chocolate, shoes, and good books. But they had never been in the same place at once.

Until one lucky weekend in New Orleans.

There was much walking and sightseeing. There were beignets and hurricanes and Voodoo shops. Plans were made and projects were started. Copious amounts of writing occurred. Amazing food was consumed. Much laughter filled the air. There may have been wine involved.

Okay, there may have been a lot of wine involved.

Somewhere during the work and play and fun, they decided they needed to write about New Orleans. "It'll be fun! We should all include three secret words! Let's call it Nine Nights in New Orleans!"

And so it happened.

Welcome to our tribute to friendship, romantic fiction, and New Orleans!

Available at Amazon and All Romance eBook

About the Author

PG Forte inhabits a world only slightly less strange than the ones she creates. Filled with serendipity, coincidence, love at first sight and dreams come true…it also bears an uncanny resemblance to Berkeley, California.

She wrote her first serialized story when she was still in her teens. The sexy, ongoing adventure tales were very popular at her oh-so-proper, all girls, Catholic High School, where they helped to liven up otherwise dull classes. Even if her teachers didn't always think so.

Originally a Jersey girl, PG now resides on the extreme left coast where she writes rule bending, genre blending erotic romance and paranormal stories.

When she's not pestering her husband to help her research scenes for upcoming books, she can usually be found serving the needs and whims of her characters….or her dog. It's a difficult job, but someone's got to do it.

Links to reach PG Forte:

www.PGForte.com
Facebook.com/AuthorPGForte
Twitter.com/PGForte

Excerpt: Finders Keepers
By PG Forte (Loose Id LLC)

Sometimes finding what you want is the easy part…

*Caleb is a bionic soldier with little-to-no memory of his past.
Aldo's an undercover cop who's searching for the man who got
away. Then there's Sally, an ER physician who used to be married
to Aldo's late partner, Davis. Sally's just looking for a reason to
keep on getting up every day.*

*This holiday season, chance will bring them together and give
them an opportunity to help one another find what they each want
most. But every gift comes with a price. And keeping what they've
found once they've found it? Yeah, that's gonna be the hard part.*

Detective Aldo Nash could almost hear his brain
humming as it worked to categorize the myriad scents
tingeing the cool night air: cedar and sea spray, dry asphalt,
cooling car engine, and most potent of all, the warm,
aroused flesh of the man Aldo had pinned beneath him.

Aldo slid practiced hands over the slim, partially clad
form, and the man moaned softly in response, his whole
body writhing instinctively closer as he arched into Aldo's
touch. Aldo pulled in another heady lungful and smiled in
contentment. On nights like these, he purely loved his job.

He couldn't say working undercover for the Oakland PD
had exactly been a lifelong dream, but Aldo's brief stint in
the army had left him uniquely qualified for it all the same,
and largely unqualified for anything else. When the USA
was formally dissolved following the economic collapse of
the 2010s and what was left of the military was fully
privatized, the idea of patriotism lost its meaning. Losing
Kyle on top of that had left Aldo with no clear idea of what
he wanted to do with his life.

After giving college a try, Aldo had signed up for the police academy on a whim. Unexpectedly, he found his niche. Now he derived a lot of satisfaction from knowing he was working to prevent future crimes from happening, not just solving those that had already occurred. He got to be proactive, stay one step ahead of the bad guys rather than the other way around. But the bottom line was proficiency. He was damned good at what he did.

Not to take away from any natural ability to dissemble he might have inherited from his late actress mother, but most of his success was due, in no small part, to all the experimental drugs he'd been given by the military. His consciousness had been purposely and methodically expanded, and his brain reconfigured to the point where he could easily exert control over his brain waves and sympathetic nervous system.

In a world where just about every criminal, from the *capo dei capi* of large, multinational drug cartels to the lowliest of hood-grown thugs, had their own psi-ops tech on speed dial, that kind of advantage was a definite point in Aldo's favor. No matter how skillful said techs might be at worming their way into other people's minds and tunneling through their thoughts, with him they could only read what he wanted them to read.

Of course, there were also things about his job he didn't like. The hours were murder since, apparently, crime rarely slept and when it did, its schedule was crap. The regular debriefings with their in-no-way-optional mind-scrubs were a major headache. Literally. Worst of all, the company he was forced to keep generally sucked, and not in that good kind of way.

That wasn't the case at the moment, however. No, when it came to his present company, Aldo had absolutely no cause for complaint. Tonight's operation had him working in tandem with a new partner, an agent on temporary loan from some alphabet agency; Aldo wasn't sure which one. He hadn't asked. He didn't care. As far as he was concerned, it didn't matter. They were all pretty much the same, and the agent would be gone soon either way. Unless Aldo had missed his guess—a possibility he considered most unlikely—his new partner had been chosen for this assignment based solely on his looks. And Aldo was certainly not unhappy with those either.

He had no idea how much of the other man's appearance was due to surgical alteration or chemical enhancement, but that was something else he sure as hell didn't care about. Hot was hot, and Special Agent Caleb Mitchell was just about the hottest thing Aldo had seen in a good long while.

Standing at a hair under six feet, Caleb was just a couple of inches shorter than Aldo. He had fair hair, full lips, broad shoulders atop a dancer's slim build, and everything about him, from his features to his proportions, was a little too perfect to be real. If the man had a flaw anywhere, Aldo had yet to find it, and not for any lack of searching. Even though they were both pushing forty, only Aldo looked his age. Special Agent Mitchell had obviously been the recent recipient of some highly classified and no doubt heavily restricted cell de-aging therapy, giving him the appearance of a man a good two decades younger than his current chronological age, the lucky bastard.

On second thought, maybe it was Aldo who'd lucked out; he got to look at the bastard, after all.

It was the case the two men were working that had brought them here tonight, to this exclusive private club located high in the Oakland Hills. Aldo's role in Operation Midas—the elaborate sting the department was running—was to attempt to infiltrate a notorious local group of wealthy, degenerate scumbags. His appearance at tonight's function, and the apparent arrest that—if everything went as planned—would shortly follow, was supposed to give him the "street cred" he needed in order to gain the scumbags' trust and acceptance. Disguised as yet another degenerate wannabe, Aldo had done his best all evening to ingratiate himself with the crew. Agent Mitchell, by virtue of his rent boy looks, had been picked to play the part of Aldo's paid escort or, as Aldo had jokingly told him, to do as he was told and look pretty doing it. He was playing his part very well, in Aldo's considered opinion, particularly at the moment.

Another gust of air blew across the parking lot. The body stretched beneath Aldo's shivered, but was it in response to the sudden chill or to the press of Aldo's fingers that had just breached his opening? Aldo leaned in closer, partially in an attempt to shield Caleb from the cool, night air, partially for the pleasure of pressing himself more firmly against that delectable flesh. "Whattsa matter, darling?" he whispered playfully in the other man's ear. "Cold?"

Caleb—bent over the hood of the shiny-new Mercedes Aldo had requisitioned for tonight's operation—glanced up at him and scowled. "Fuck you, Nash. Skip the chitchat, all right? Let's just get this over with." Up until that moment, Aldo had found Caleb's permanently raspy voice a big turn-on, but there was nothing sexy about that angry tone, the gritted teeth, the fury blazing in those jade-green eyes.

Loose Id: http://www.loose-id.com/finders-keepers-1.html
Also available at Amazon, Barnes & Noble and All Romance eBooks.

Excerpt: Let Me Count the Ways
By PG Forte (Liquid Silver Books)

When former film star Claire Calhoun picks up her accountant, Mike Sherman, after a party one night she's thinking fling. He's thinking forever.

Claire has been Mike's fantasy since the first time he saw her. Now that she's in his bed, he'll do whatever is necessary to keep her there. But he's not a stalker, right? He's just a devoted fan.

Prologue

Mike

I guess you could say I fell for Claire Calhoun the first time I saw her up there on the big silver screen. I don't know what it was about her that affected me so strongly. Maybe it was the Titan hair. The sultry shimmer in those hazel, hellcat eyes. The curve of her lips when she turned and smiled right at the camera--right at me. Whatever it was, it was simply...stunning. Literally. It hit me hard and low and just wouldn't quit.

She looked like an angel with all that California sunshine spilling down around her; like sweet, lust-inducing innocence dipped in honey. A vision straight from some Garden of Earthly Delights.

But if her face was made for heaven, everything south of that had been built with a far different destination in mind. Her body was sinful enough to tempt even a saint into straying. Happily. Right through the gates of Hell. And I'm far from being a saint.

Despite my on-going fascination with the woman, I'd just like to state for the record that I never deluded myself into believing we had a relationship. Claire could have been as fictional as any of the characters she played for all the good I figured it was ever going to do me. There had to be at least a million other guys in the world who wanted her as badly as I did and I knew any number of them were more likely than I to even meet her. Not that it stopped me from dreaming, of course. But dreaming, fantasizing, collecting memorabilia--along with copies of every one of her films I could get my hands on--that's as far as it went.

For a while, Claire's name was box office magic. Everything she touched turned golden. But then a string of unsuccessful movies and even less successful relationships caused her star to plummet. These days, her screen appearances are mostly limited to round-ups subtitled 'Where are They Now?'

To me, however, Claire would always be a major star, a full blown fantasy, a lush and lovely dream come true. Which is why I could scarcely believe my eyes the day she walked into my office hoping to secure my services as accountant to her new exercise studio, The Body Electric.

To say I was star-struck in her presence was understating the case by a very, very wide margin. I was hopelessly tongue tied, socially inept, and all but physically impaired by the kind of hard-on most men my age have given up expecting to achieve without pharmaceutical assistance. It still surprises me that we both made it through that first meeting; that I didn't embarrass myself any worse than I had; that she didn't bolt for the door after spending less than five minutes in my bumbling presence.

Luckily for me, I had come highly recommended by Claire's attorney, Dave Gillen. Dave, who'd recently extricated Claire from marriage number six and brokered the deal that allowed her to walk away with enough money to start her business in the first place, was also one of my oldest clients.

Claire trusted Dave, Dave trusted me, and the rest, as they say, is history...

Liquid Silver: http://www.lsbooks.com/let-me-count-the-ways-p349.php
Also available at Amazon, Barnes & Noble and All Romance eBooks.

Excerpt: Scent of the Roses
By PG Forte (SynergEbooks)

There's something magical about the tiny coast town of Oberon, California…

When a slumber party prank goes awry, magical forces are unleashed that will forever alter the lives of four teenaged girls. Twenty years later, Scout Patterson has returned to Oberon in search of answers. What she finds instead are lies and betrayal…and a second chance at her first love.

But Scout's homecoming is followed by a reoccurrence of deadly attacks, and officer Nick Greco must rush to solve an all-but-forgotten crime or risk losing her again – this time for good.

They took their drinks out to the patio while they waited for the pizza, and if Scout thought that being out of the house would be an improvement, she quickly realized her mistake. Her younger self had imagined scenes like this one far too many times...

There would be music playing, and the two of them would be right here on the sun-warmed bricks of the patio, with the hot tub, and the Mexican ceramic fireplace, and the large, old, Royal Palm tree strung with tiny white lights.

She'd turned on the lights tonight almost without thinking, and the stereo as well. And now, she felt almost as though she'd entered one of her own fantasies. Except that the hot tub had always figured a little more prominently in most of those fantasies.

Nick was standing a slight distance away from her, leaning on the railing, taking in the view. She found her own gaze returning, again and again, to his profile. She swallowed hard, and wrenched her eyes away, once more forcing herself to focus on the larger view, instead.

She had filled the bird feeders early that morning in a fit of enthusiasm, and now, what seemed like dozens of house finches darted and swooped across the yard. Two of the cats, sitting motionless on the deck, watched them through narrowed eyes. The gardens, always lush with flowers anyway, positively shimmered as the slanting rays of the sun glinted off the wings of the butterflies and hummingbirds that fluttered around the blossoms. The mingled scents of honeysuckle, jasmine and rose was almost overpowering.

To the left of the yard rose the dark, graceful woods, through which she used to travel back and forth to school. And in the distance, partially obscured, a sliver of ocean view could be glimpsed--sparkling, pure shot silver-- between the large, old bay laurel trees that bordered the property line at the back. It was impossibly romantic, Scout thought, with a flash of irritation. It was completely, totally and unfairly romantic. Just like all those fantasies...

The golden sun gilding everything it touched, the soft sounds of bird calls, the perfumed air. And Nick. Looking so impossibly good.

Oh, God help her, she was staring at him again. But she just couldn't help herself. There were those soft curls at the nape of his neck where they just brushed against his collar. And his arms, so strong and tanned- How could you look at arms like that, and not wonder how it would feel to have them wrapped around you? The problem was, she remembered all too well what it felt like. And she wanted to feel it again.

Forget it, a harsh voice in her head kept saying. *That was years ago. He doesn't care now. Hasn't he made that perfectly clear? He's moved on with his life. Why can't you?*

Scout took another sip of her Shiraz. The smooth, peppery coolness slid down her throat to turn warm in her stomach. And all the while, a smaller, softer voice continued insisting, *He did care, once. I bet I could make him care, again.*

SynergEbooks:
http://www.synergebooks.com/ebook_scentoftheroses.htm
l
Also available at Amazon, Barnes & Noble and All Romance
eBooks.